ALL P

The Inside Story of Italia '90

PETE DAVIES

FourFourTwo

For Joe

who at the age of eight months just got his first football

First published in Great Britain in 1990 by William Heinemann Ltd.

First published by Yellow Jersey Press in 1998
Abridged by Yellow Jersey Press for *FourFourTwo*

Yellow Jersey Press
Random House, 20 Vauxhall Bridge Road,
London SW1V 2SA

Random House Australia (Pty) Limited
20 Alfred Street, Milsons Point, Sydney,
New South Wales 2061, Australia

Random House New Zealand Limited
18 Poland Road, Glenfield,
Auckland 10, New Zealand

Random House South Africa (Pty) Limited
Endulini, 5A Jubilee Road, Parktown 2193,
South Africa

The Random House Group Limited Reg. No. 954009
www.randomhouse.co.uk

A CIP catalogue record for this book
is available from the British Library

ISBN 0 224 07549 7

Papers used by Random House are natural, recyclable products made from wood grown in sustainable forests. The manufacturing processes conform to the environmental regulations of the country of origin

Printed and bound in Great Britain by
Cox & Wyman Ltd, Reading, Berkshire

Sardinian Cavalcades

Welcome to Cagliari

Mario Mariosardara, known to one and all simply as Marius, is a slightly stout, bow-legged, and cheerful man, looking very well indeed on his sixty-odd years. He's the chairman of the Cagliari supporter's club, and his bar – the Bar Marius on the junction of Viale Trieste and Viale Trento – is a shrine, a veritable temple to the great and good god Football.

We met in April, at a conference called 'Arrivano Gli Inglesi': 'The English Are Coming'. It had been called to consider how Cagliari might best prepare itself for the most feared fans in the Mondiale – but as far as Marius was concerned, the English were welcome. He had a big banner put up in his bar to say so; and among the pictures of his local heroes on the shelf behind the chrome counter, he added for the occasion a signed photograph of Gary Lineker.

After the conference, the British Council gave us dinner at Il Corsaro, on Viale Regina Margherita. I sat on Marius' right, and on his left was Tom Finney. Marius talked about the weather – a serious business in Sardinia, where it had pretty much given up raining for three years, so that farmers had dire troubles, and in my *pensione* you could only shower in the mornings – and we talked about football, and fans, and about life in general.

But with metronomic regularity, Marius's conversation was punctuated at ten-minute intervals with sudden happy little sighs of disbelief: 'I can't believe I'm sitting next to the great Tom Finney.' He'd smile a little smile, like he'd just woken up in heaven and decided, after due deliberation, that he liked it, he liked it very much; he'd then say quietly again, 'The great Tom Finney . . .'

Finney at the conference told a nice little story. Back when £12 a week was the maximum wage, the manager at his club (Preston North End) called him in at the end of the season and said, as always, that they'd like to keep him – and the wage would be, as always, £12 a week, with £10 a week in the summer. Next in was Tommy Docherty, and the manager said he too would have £12 a week – but only £8 a week in the summer.

'No,' says Docherty, 'I want what Finney's getting.'

'But Finney's a better player than you.'

'Not in the summer he's not.'

Tom Finney . . . third equal with thirty goals on the England all-time scoring list with Nat Lofthouse and, since his goal against Brazil a month earlier, who else but Gary Lineker. Marius, an absolute fan, sat and smiled through the multi-course spectacular, and said over and over how he couldn't believe he was sitting next to the great Tom Finney.

Gary Lineker, of course, makes a bit more than £12 a week.

Bobby Robson ate in Il Corsaro some months before the draw for the World Cup in Rome on 9 December 1989 . . . In their qualifying group, England at that time still needed two points from away games in Stockholm and Katowice – but the Italians knew where they'd be sending the English if they got those two points: Quarantine Camp Cagliari. The secretary of the local organising committee, Roberto Pappalardo, whose family owned most of the cinemas on Sardinia, told me it had been known for six months in advance of the draw that if they qualified, then England would be there.

Because these were not the glory days of Tom Finney. These, it seemed, were the new horror days of a nation that was all played out, a nation of riot and yobbery, a nation whose football was oafish and whose fans were louts, a nation with a ridiculous government, an economy in a tailspin, food you daren't eat and weather you daren't go out in . . . England, England, whatever the hell happened to England? The arrival of its team and their brute following would have to be planned for a year in advance – though as we shall see, advance preparation in Italy's not a thing that runs to any fixed or recognisable schedule . . .

Marius didn't see it that way. At the conference he said that he'd been following football for fifty years, and if there was a great deal of alarm developing over England's presence on the island, himself, he could see little reason for that. And – despite the shrill fear and loathing of their newspapers, banging on and on about hooligans until the very word became synonymous with English – a sizeable proportion of the other good people of Cagliari seemed to feel the same way. English football is held in higher esteem abroad than it is at home; for Marius, and for many others, England playing three World Cup matches in Cagliari was just *great*. It was, I'd estimate, the fourth best thing in Marius's life as a fan.

The third best thing would have been Italy winning the World Cup in Spain in 1982 – a moment when, some say, Italy felt truly united as a nation for the first time in its 130-year history, with the much-loved then-President Sandro Pertini leaping to his feet in ecstasy and abandon beside King Juan Carlos in the VIP box. (I'm reckoning that as the titles of '34 and '38 occurred during the forced unity of the Mussolini time, they can't be held to count in the same way.)

But I don't doubt that the first best thing for Marius would have been when Cagliari won the national league championship in 1970. It was in honour of this triumph that the Bar Marius had been made into a shrine, with many huge, grainy, black-and-white photos, and even a statue, of the winning side's great man Gigi Riva, along with flags and pennants, and every other imaginable kind of memento.

It was after this victory that the Stadio Sant'Elia was built, to accommodate the club's new ambitions. But unfortunately, things didn't work out the way the people of Cagliari had hoped; in the following years they slipped back into grief and relegation. In 1971 Italy played Spain in Cagliari, and made the enormously tactless blunder of not selecting any members of the previous year's championship winners; in the Great Orange Riot, the national side was harried off the field by furious Outspan-hurling locals.

No more internationals were played in Cagliari for the next eighteen years – until, on 21 December 1989, Italy came back to the forgotten island, and drew a friendly 0–0 with Argentina. By all accounts this match was so dreary, the Sards could probably have done without it – even Bobby Robson, congenitally cautious in public, said the game was 'very disappointing' – but it did mark an important return to recognition for Cagliari. And with the World Cup coming their way, they were halfway through a season whose end would bring the second best thing in Marius's life as a fan: promotion back into Serie A, the Italian First Division.

It was a very fine way to kick off your World Cup, and on 3 June 1990, it was to celebrate this that we gathered at the Bar Marius.

The bar itself was theoretically shut, though a handful of us did limbo our way under the door grille that was levered up a metre off the floor, to get ourselves a preliminary beer or two. I snatched a glance at a triumphal edition of one of the local papers, *L'Unione Sarda*: 'Cagliari In A', cried the headline, 'Back To The Future!' Now, from the pit of C, from years of suffering and humiliation as in Dante's *Inferno*, a return to the celestial music of A – it was new life, it was renaissance, it was joy unconfined and unending . . .

Cagliari are the *rossoblu*, the red and blues – and every one of the cars gathering outside was either covered in flags in those colours, or simply painted in them for good. There were two flatbeds to head the procession, both trailers crammed with crazy souls with their faces made up in *rossoblu*, wearing *rossoblu* ostrich-feather headgear. They had drums and hooters, cymbals and horns. There were guys with wonderfully hideous red spangly jackets, and equally awful gold spangly top hats; there were guys with blacked faces wearing garish gauze *rossoblu* dresses, and girls of a positively unearthly beauty riding the bonnets of cars in *rossoblu* pixie suits. There were *rossoblu* caps, seed hats, headbands and scarves. Pictures of the team were taped to car doors and windows; makeshift wooden 'A's painted *rossoblu* stood proud on the roofs of this motley vehicle jamboree, and big 'A's were sewn on to the shirts of the girls. There were women and kids everywhere among the boys, the *rossoblu ragazzi*; and there were police cars and bikes, ready to shepherd the hooting convoy on its way all round town.

I rode in the cab of the lead truck, and when we began there were maybe thirty cars; but that number grew until they stretched as far back as I could see, and then further. Listening to snatches of commentary on the radio from Cagliari's last game, away to Messina – not that the result mattered any more – we set off at a crawl in a cloud of *rossoblu* confetti, past a babe in her mother's arms waving a *rossoblu* pennant, west on to Viale Sant'Avendrace.

A man in an orange and white lace skirt yelled from the trailer behind me for regular updates from Messina. We tossed little tags of paper out the windows that fluttered up and away in the wind on to the streets, the tags printed on one side with the name of the club president, and on the other with the name of a brand of coffee. A three-wheeler van cruised alongside us, sporting custom-made *rossoblu* skirts. We forked right on to the climb up Via San Michele, and looped back towards the heart of the town along Via Is Mirrionis. People threw plastic *rossoblu* pennants off the flatbeds to all the children who scampered beside us as we went on our deafening drumming way, and, clutching footballs and flags, they ran cheering beside us until their mothers scooped them up. Pairs of boys on scooters raced back and forth around and between the cars, one steering (if you can call it that) while the pillion riders waved vast banners. In windows and on balconies people called out and applauded, and were clapped back in return.

And so we made our way across the back of the intricate medieval centre, perched around the Arsenal and the Castello with their views over the broad bay, the Gulf of Angels. Cagliari – Italy's seventh biggest port, and the principal port and city of Sardinia – sprawls as a peculiar agglomerate of ill-connected districts, many sprung up since the town was bombed heavily in the war. The city's quarter of a million people now find space to build wherever the hard geography of rock and brackish marsh will let them. It's not the prettiest place on earth – it's an unpretentious working port, with the ready humour such towns tend to have – but it's far from being the ugliest, and if you treat it right it's friendly and warm. And it does like its football . . .

We passed under the enormous and imposing San Remy Bastion, through the twisty old shopping district – Via Manno had (of course) a World Cup promotion going on, with a large model of the mascot, Ciao, mysteriously suspended in a perspex globe – and then we came to the sea down the wide slope of Largo Carlo Felice, under the walls of the medieval heart, and the heavy mass of the Elephant Tower. We turned left on Via Roma, the grand harbour-front avenue, with ferries from the mainland, and Korean and Yugoslavian freighters, all wedged together under the cranes to our right.

To our left, under the solid and shuttered four-storey facades painted, eclectically, lilac and cream, mauve and maroon, ran the long arcade with the Caffe Torino and the Caffe Roma – places that would soon be gathering points for the more visible variety of England fan. Along this arcade, too, stroll the youth of Cagliari – hardly a gilded lot, but graced, certainly, with some of the best-looking girls I ever saw in my life. The guy driving my truck kept leaning out and calling to them, 'Hey, wanna ride? Wanna ride in my cab? Wanna sample some English cock I got in here?'

We were *en route* to the stadium now, the last stretch of our two-hour Sardinian cavalcade. By the time we were passing the Stadio Amsicora – Cagliari's previous ground, now home to a successful hockey side – the procession involved literally hundreds of cars, packed three wide so the main road out of town was blocked solid by a hooting, parping, gear-grinding mass, the whole thing stretching back hundreds and hundreds of metres under an ocean of flags. It can't have done much good for the greenhouse effect – but it was certainly fun.

Then everyone unfurled off the road into chaos in a vast parking lot; the armada broke up, some headed for the beach at Poetto, and others back home. I got out and stumbled around among the celebrants, bewildered and grinning. I said to one guy I vaguely knew, 'That was great.'

'Oh,' he said, 'that was nothing, that was tiny. You should have seen us last week when we were playing at home.'

I thought, if this is what happens when they get promoted to Serie A – what happens if they win the World Cup?

And what happens *if they lose*?

The Sunday before, Bobby Robson went to Cagliari's last home game, against Triestina.

I'd watched Cagliari at the Sant'Elia myself, back in April – they beat Padova 1–0. In England, obviously, you'd need to stick a roof on the place – not being rich in rain, Cagliari has little need of one – but apart from that, I can't think of many

First Division clubs that wouldn't swap everything in an instant for a home like this ground (if they had any sense, which is, of course, not a definite assumption). But it is, anyhow, a simple two-tiered bowl, it seats 40,000, and it's splendid.

Even with only 15,000 in it for the Padova game, it was still a sight more lively than most Second Division fixtures you could think of in England. The cheap seats in the upper tier of the Curva Nord where the lads, the *ragazzi*, all sit, was a packed throng of *rossoblu*, with their banners strung the whole length of the rim of the tier. The banners read, FURIOSI, EAGLES, ULTRA CAGLIARI, BRIGATA S. ELIA, CRAZY BOYS, BUNKER SKiN, and SCONVOLTS – for which an appromixate slang translation would be, HEADCASES. And when the team came out, so did a torrent of *rossoblu* smoke flares.

Equally different was the quality of the play – notably in defence, where the ball was never hoofed out, but always *played* out, even off the by-line. When, under pressure, the Padova defenders did turf it up the field, they were heartily jeered for this inelegance. Anchored by the sweeper, the defenders were confidently mobile, and comfortable going forward. The first time I noticed the Cagliari keeper kicking the ball upfield, rather than throwing it out to the feet of his back men, was in the eighty-second minute.

Since first I met him, this had been a main strand of Robson's conversation – that on the Continent, 'the defenders can all play'. And where could he get him some defenders like that?

For now, I don't know what he thought of Cagliari's defence. I only know that when he and some of his players went to watch that last home game in a packed, promoted, and partymood Sant'Elia on 27 May (seeking support and PR, sure, but also out of courtesy to his island hosts) he was pleasantly greeted, and he enjoyed himself. He asked wryly, 'Is it like this every Sunday?' – which became a headline in *L'Unione Sarda* the next day. He saw, said the local paper, 'a stadium in delirium'; and while the paper admitted that the 40,000 had other things on their minds, nonetheless the introduction of the English players on the pitch did create 'a certain feeling', and Robson himself had 'a serene afternoon'.

And I know, too, that since the party was packed, there was no room for the English press. But a photographer from the *Sun* told a reporter from the Press Association that Robson had been booed and jeered; and in no time at all this falsehood was headed back to London down the wires with all the others.

Meanwhile, back to 3 June and the breaking up of the cavalcade. I went from there with many others to Poetto, where an exceptionally pleasant white sand beach lies along the Gulf of Quartu, looking out to the next rung of coastal hills, tinted now a pastel pink-orange in the slow-falling sunset. Many flags from the procession had become goalposts, and kids played between them on the beach. At the south end of the shore, boats lay moored under the Devil's Saddle, a stony bolster of crag and pinnacle tumbling steeply down into the sea; to the north, the beach splintered up into a tacky strand of resort cafés, and an amusement park.

Cars still paraded on the coast road in their *rossoblu* livery. At some point an ambulance came, which was probably inevitable. The Italians have such an absurdly high danger threshold – boys and girls waving flags on the roofs and bonnets of their cars, bouncing along the rutted and bumpy beach lanes – that sooner or later, someone was bound to come off.

But the bulk of the people had long since gathered on the beach, for a final promotion party and concert. The band played Euro-pop – lyrics in English, predictably – and there was a new Cagliari anthem. In the deepening dusk the growing audience, with their myriad flags and banners – the colours of the club, of the city, and of the island – looked like nothing so much as a medieval army, a mass of people on the shore under a fluttering ocean of heraldic emblems and symbols on a ground of *rossoblu*.

A medieval army – drinking cans of Heineken, and eating the tastiest hot dogs I ever had in my life . . . There are those who say that football, in Italy, is a continuation of war between the medieval city states by other means. And certainly, Sardinia is not like the rest of that country at all.

Sardinia, people told me, was the first piece of Europe to

rise from the waves. True or not, the geology of the place looks weird and fantastical. Great wind-worn lumps of contorted grey rock lie scattered along the edge of the turquoise sea; there's one called 'The Dinosaur', and another – perfect dirty postcard material – shaped exactly like an enormous erect penis.

People have been on Sardinia since the time of the Nuragic civilisation, at least 4,000 years ago. But different invaders have swept one after another across these antique shores, so that Cagliari is not a typical Sard settlement at all. Sardinian towns, more typically, are small places tucked away from danger in the rugged folds of the interior, suspicious and isolated – while all around the coast stands a ring of ninety-nine stone watchtowers, put up by the Spanish when it was their turn to be boss.

The shield of this singular island has four black blindfolded heads, one in each quarter of a white background split by a red cross; but what's doubly singular about it is that it's not actually Sardinian at all. The blindfolds were originally headbands; the heads were an emblem of the King of Aragon, and date back to 1281. The Aragonese occupied Sardinia in 1323, and the emblem was then mistakenly ascribed to the island by a Dutch king compiling an early guide to heraldry. Then later, in the nineteenth century, the headbands began to slip . . . so that even the symbol of Sardinia is not what it seems. Sardinia, in short, is a place very much unto itself – its private soul kept private behind other people's languages, and other people's governments.

It's been occupied by Phoenicians and Romans, Vandals and Goths, Moors and Pisans, Aragonese and Savoyards – so, after all, what kind of difficulty could a couple of weeks' worth of English fans ever present?

Some days later, I hitched a ride back into Cagliari along the forty kilometres of coast road from Is Molas, the England squad's hotel, with an amiable farmer in a disintegrating and manure-smeared old Fiat. 'What,' he asked, 'is all this rumpus in the papers about hooligans? Where are they? What's the problem?' He was one of that growing band of souls who, sadly, feel they must now instinctively distrust every word that they read.

'But,' he said, 'if there are hooligans, you tell them from

me. We are not a tourist trap here, we are not interested in the size of your wallet. You be friendly with us, we be friendly with you. But if you do cause trouble, be sure. If we get to you before the police do, all the policemen will find is a corpse.'

My second Sardinian cavalcade came on 5 June, two days after the promotion parade, and it was a very different business altogether. It was a ride that took us a big distance further into the unreality zone; it was a bewildering vision of what, on Planet Football, the care and management of a national team now involves.

England's last game, before they opened Group F against Ireland on 11 June, was a kick-about friendly with a scratch Sardinian Select XI in Oristano, a hundred kilometres north of Cagliari. (At the end of May they'd beaten Cagliari 6–0 on the training ground at Pula, which, after the FA's PR men took half-page ads in the local papers to congratulate Cagliari on promotion, might be thought a little tactless . . . but then, like they say, there's no sentiment in football.)

This second friendly at Oristano was slated originally for Porto Torres or Sassari at the other end of the island; but the security implications of the squad travelling four or more hours either way – let alone the drain on the players – soon put paid to that. Instead, Stefano Arrica, the son of a big man in the Cagliari club, organised a job lot of local third and fourth division players in forty-eight hours; a job lot graced by local boy Gianfranco Zola, Maradona's understudy at Napoli, who was back at home on holiday.

It was an enjoyable afternoon, made more so by the bleak and baked beauty of the journey, and by the company I had on the outward leg of it. I was driven to the game by the War Correspondent of *Il Giorno* – a charming and drily witty man who, since he'd covered Vietnam, the Congo, the Gulf War, Central America and the Lebanon, got told by his paper, 'You're just the man for Cagliari.' And we talked about a host of things . . .

On Maradona: 'A very stupid human being – a simple-minded slum boy.'

On wars: 'Vietnam was a beautiful war. The Americans provided such splendid facilities . . .' Except he hadn't enjoyed filling in the form to say who'd pay, if he got sent home in a bag.

And on Sardinia, which he loved, and where he often took his holidays: 'This is a bad choice for England. These are a very strange and violent people. In Greece in World War II the Germans and the Italians were marching on Athens, and one Sardinian boy took pity on the people, and gave his bread to a woman with a baby. A German said to him, "You must show no weakness," and punched the boy. So the boy jumped on the German's chest and killed him – with his head. Some of the villages here, you see – the annual festival includes a headbutting party. They run full on into metal doors with their foreheads . . .'

When the Germans and the Austrians defeated the Italians at Caporetto in World War I, the 5,000 men of the Sardinian Brigata Sassari earned undying fame. Entire divisions tried to pass them and failed, until the Sards had lost eighty per cent of their men. 'They are very stubborn. You go see them in the mountains – if you're good friends with a man, you might speak ten words with him in a day.'

Generally in Italy, he said, the great majority of kidnap victims survive. But when Sards are involved, that's not necessarily so. The victims disappear. 'They feed them to their pigs.'

In Cagliari there were, he said, two very hard areas. There was Sant'Elia, 'where everyone's been to jail'. And then there was another district where the working people live, a lot of whom used to be miners, though of course the mines are all shut now. 'These people – they are very good with dynamite.'

I think the War Correspondent enjoyed himself, spinning these tales. After all, I met with nothing but friendliness on Sardinia. But then, he was not like the joke-named 'war correspondents' sent out by the English tabloids to report on fan violence – and, if there wasn't any, to make some up. He was an honest man who, as the tournament unfolded, grew steadily more convinced that for the most part the English, in fact, were behaving just fine . . .

After an hour or so, we came through a vent in the moonscape, and a yellow-brown plain, broiling in heat haze, yawned open before us. We could tell where Oristano was by the helicopter hovering over the arrival of the squad in the distance. The town itself was a dull-looking place of squat square buildings, all breezeblock and dust – but you don't go to Sardinia for the architecture. (The finest things in Cagliari, like the Duomo, were built by the Pisans in the thirteenth century.)

We caught up with the team bus in a flurry of police cars and motorbikes. 'Nothing,' said the War Correspondent, 'will ever have happened in Oristano like this.' The road to the little ground was sealed off.

The ground itself was shabby but homely, with two small stands along either side of the pitch, one of them roofed. There were maybe 3,000 locals there – not, of course, 'strange and violent' at all, but thoroughly relaxed, and pleased about the odd spectacle they were about to enjoy. There were also daft numbers of policemen, keeping a benign eye on the twenty or thirty England lads who'd come up from Cagliari by bus or train for the day.

Some English press grumbled – out of habit, basically – that they were morons and deadheads, when they acted up for the cameras. I made a note, 'You only sing when they're filming' – but why shouldn't they? Why point the bloody cameras at them in the first place? One of the tabloid men (morons, deadheads) called them 'professional hooligans' – a nice way to talk about your readers . . . But I'd met these boys already back in Cagliari, and, if they weren't the brightest in the world, there was no malevolence about them. All they wanted was a fun afternoon – and England sure gave them one.

First, however, players and FA men went around the crowd, giving lollipops to children. They were whoppers, maybe three inches in diameter, and they said 'FIFA World Cup – England – Italy 1990'. Kids slurped on them contentedly; a couple of Red Cross ladies chattered in front of me that it was a nice thing to do.

Then the game kicked off, with a rather more ham-fisted little piece of PR. From the whistle, McMahon took the ball straight back down the pitch, and scored a deliberate own goal. We had an FA press release saying this was a message to fans, that violence was an own goal so please don't score one – but the immediate result was 3,000 exceedingly bewildered Sardinians. Had the heat got to McMahon here, or what?

Still, giving them a 1–0 lead in the first minute didn't mean a whole lot with Steve Bull on the park. He went up the other end and, in the second minute, he made it 1–1. By half-time, it was 5–1.

It was a muggy day, and the overcast sky began to drip the odd speck of unfamiliar rain – otherwise, the second half looked more or less the same as the first. Seaman, taking his turn in goal, missed a twenty-five yard shot that made it 5–2 (though his World Cup was soon to end in more sadness than he'd have felt over that little slip) and then normal business was resumed. The game finished 10–2.

Twenty or twenty-five English pressmen gathered in a circle round Robson on the pitch – Robson turned on one of them stood behind him, whose paper had been laying on some Grade A vitriol lately, and said, 'I don't want *you* where I can't see you.'

I don't see how anyone would have learnt too much. The England lads, mightily amused by their team's afternoon, chanted sporadically from the stand, but found it a bit hard to work out who to sing for. Only one Peter Beardsley? Only one Steve Bull? Only one Sardinia Select?

Outside, small crowds of *ragazzi* gathered to cheer the England bus away. My War Correspondent had vanished, so, seeing Jane Nottage from the Italia '90 Press Office, I hitched a ride in the cavalcade instead. And, rather abruptly, a gentle kick-about in Nowheresville turned back into the fourteenth World Cup.

At first there was the customary swirling mayhem of police cars and bikes, edging their way through the knots of friendly kids; among them, the *scooteristas* weaved back and forth round the throng of our vehicles as the engines grumbled, and the sirens began. Then, slowly, the motorcade fanned out and lined up – and long before we'd left Oristano I'd started thinking, this isn't real life, *this is a movie*.

At the front were two *carabinieri* cars, then a regular police car. Next came the team bus, and the team van for any spare local or FA officials. Then there was a plainclothes car, and after that two Italia '90 cars. Then there followed another *carabinieri* car, a blue bus filled with yet more *carabinieri*, two armoured police vehicles, and two more plainclothes cars. Add to these fourteen vehicles a brace of perpetually siren-blowing outriders (you know the kind of guys, heavy black boots, and seriously dark LA-style gold-rimmed shades) cruising back and forth the whole length of the noisy parade, steering with one hand, waving traffic off our lane with fluorescent red wands in the other, and you have a truly grandiose spectacle.

But still we weren't safe enough. As we came out on to the parched plain, the eerie lunar mountains rising to either side of us, the police helicopter appeared again, and clattered into place up above us. And, describing a circling string of loops to stay in place overhead, it stuck with us the whole length of the journey back home.

So, passing through this strange and savage terrain, past unfenced fields of bleached grain stretched out under jagged, stone-strewn stacks of ridge and rough peak, I thought, just a minute here. Who's in that bus? Bush? Gorby? This month's Italian government? Nah – it's a football team . . .

One of twenty-four such teams who were, for these few weeks, the most important people on the face of the earth – their comings and goings, their passes and tackles, their fouls and their injuries and their goals and their dreams all monitored by thousands of journalists, and eagerly scanned by the billions on TV.

So important, indeed, that absurdly hysterical news had now come from London that Abu Nidal, the devil his very self, was after their hides. Or, as Nottage called him, Abdul Needle. But let's face it – if he was going to do it, he wouldn't tell the tabloids.

And my main personal fear, as we careered through the moonscape, was that if Abdul Needle did opt to have a go, all these zillions of *carabinieri* would as likely as not go terminally doolally and in their panic, shoot *me*.

Ah well. In three days' time it was off to Milan, for Argentina–Cameroon . . .

All Played Out

England–Ireland

On the 9th I got an early flight back from Milan, and ran into some lively work from *L'Unione Sarda*:

BATTLE IN CAGLIARI

The story talked about 'moments of authentic urban warfare' – and there did appear to have been, in the glorious Italian phrase, a bit of *fuggi fuggi* on the streets downtown.

Hank, the Irish labourer from Kilburn, had moved into La Perla; he told me what he'd seen. He'd been sitting in the Via Roma arcade, him and other Irishmen among perhaps eighty or a hundred English. (So they can't have been the nasty mob – or the unmistakably Irish Hank wouldn't have been telling the tale the next morning.) He said some of the English were drunk – a few dead drunk and crashed out in their chairs, others dancing and singing. And some of it was noisy when it came to 'God Save the Queen' – but there were Italians stopping to watch as they passed, and they didn't seem spooked. Hank said they seemed to be enjoying it.

From about 9.00 onwards, police in riot gear started gathering across the way on the central reservation.

Hank stressed, the Sards seemed to be enjoying it. 'They must have been five deep between us and the police. They'd watch for ten or fifteen minutes, then move on, and someone else'd take their place. They were men, women, all different ages – some came in to talk with us, it was really no problem.'

But police in vans still pulled up across the road from the cafés. They put on their helmets as they got out, and thwacked their truncheons on their thighs.

'It was very threatening. And there was really no need – we

were sitting about minding our own business. At least, on the tables around me we all were. I think, if they hadn't come on like they did, nothing would have happened.'

The bars had run out of draught, but they were carrying on selling cans – and everyone was paying – they were queuing to pay. Then, as if pre-planned, the tables were cleared away; the police moved in to send people on their way.

I heard later that five minutes before they did so, an Italian TV crew turned up. Funny, that.

Hank said people went more or less peaceably – some weren't too happy about the manner of it, but there were no unduly aggressive objections. People were backed up an alley – Via Baylle – and then some idiot threw a glass.

Others told me later that the idiot in question was the mean-eyed gobshite from Harrogate.

In Stockholm when they'd chucked a glass, the Swedish police looked disgusted, and tidied it up.

In Cagliari, they charged.

Hank was at the top of Via Baylle with six or seven others. He didn't hang around to find out what happened next.

Hank said the drinks ban wouldn't mean much. People would find drink if they wanted to – or else they'd buy dope, you could get it easy anywhere. 'But they're asking daft prices, £10 for a few joints' worth. Do they think we're stupid, or what?'

After he'd got away, he went to a disco. Three Sard boys tried having a go at him – but other locals intervened, and stopped them. He left there at four, and walked the streets till six; then he sat down in the Via Roma for a couple of hours before coming back to bed when La Perla opened. Where he'd sat down – where the BATTLE IN CAGLIARI took place – the streets were 'pure clean like nothing happened'.

He said it was a pity. The Irish fans like himself would drink and have fun, then clear off to Sicily on Tuesday. But the English had to be there another two weeks – 'and they're getting trouble just for being themselves'. He said some were saying, after last night, they'd go up north. They'd bought tickets on the street, but they'd end up watching the game on TV in Alghero, or Sassari – for the sake of one jerk who threw a glass and gave the police their cue to wade in. After which, of course, other missiles would have been thrown and everyone English became guilty.

English boys told me later they'd been lined up against a wall, and given an exemplary taste of truncheon. The police told them, 'You're in Italy now.' Fourteen were arrested; a bar was reported 'devastated'.

Hank said the Sards were great. 'I'd love to stay here for six or twelve months, that's honest. If you just try and speak a little they'll help you, and they'll love you for it. And there's English trying too. And none of the English have gone after me – sure, one or two give it the IRA and that, but they're not NF, they're friendly – I turn a blind eye, I'm not here for the fight. And these English, they mix with the Irish, there's Irish here, English there, all around the tables – there were even two fellers from Norway supporting England, dressed in England gear and all. There was never any problem.'

I walked down Via Baylle, where the BATTLE IN CAGLIARI began. There were two lines of baby palm trees in pots; the alley was top-to-bottom with little clothes stores, and a jeweller's shop – and all the clothes stores had outside them on the walls the shallow, wooden, glass-fronted cases in which backstreet Italian stores display their wares.

There was no broken glass in any of the cases; no sign of damage or hooliganism of any kind whatsoever.

'We will sit here. Write that down. The pitch is not quite perfect. Write that down.'

A Teuton from FIFA came down to Cagliari to inspect things. He went to Is Morus, to ask Jack Charlton for the Irish team's programme.

The answer came back, in effect, what programme? If they felt like training they trained, and if they didn't, they didn't. Ditto talking to the press – which the players all happily did anyway.

Nottage said the Irish were unbelievable. Ten of their journalists had turned up without accreditation. But they had no complaints, and no problems – they operated with a happy conviction that everything would work out OK.

They were, in fact, rather like the Italians . . . except for the way they played football.

*

In Bologna, Colombia put two goals past the United Arab Emirates. The English referee, George Courtney, appropriately, a school headmaster, was much admired for his sang-froid. When players put on the histrionic rolls of agony, he told them to get up and get on with it – so eventually they all did. John Williams said it was a splendid and colourful afternoon, sheiks and salsa and skill – and he reported a delicious World Cup image.

There is, in Bologna, the longest covered walkway in the world, winding up the hill above the Stadio Renato Dall'Ara. And as a little old Italian lady in black went slowly up it, a Colombian kid raced past her coming down the other way, slaloming in and out of the arches with a vast flag fluttering, red, blue, and gold . . . the football festivities were under way.

In Bari, the Romanians beat the Russians 2–0 – Marius Lacatus scoring a beauty late in the first half, then putting home a dodgy penalty in the second. The ball must have been handled a good yard outside the area – but the Uruguayan referee Juan Cardellino (a salesman when he's at home) didn't see it that way.

The football was fluid, fast, athletic, and intelligent. An Italian hotelier, mindful of gruesome doings in Romania, bought tickets for a thousand of the Romanian fans.

I watched Russia–Romania in the Bar Svizzera with a printer called Radio Mitch. He'd gone to the States twelve years ago, to Philadelphia – but he hated it there, the change from summer to winter was 'thermal shock' – so he moved to Oakland, in the Bay. He loved America – but he was English to his boots.

He said, 'I hate Maradona. He's a fuckin' girl.' And when they replayed Omam Biyik's goal for Cameroon, he said of Pumpido, 'My mum could have saved that. What a fuckin' woman.'

Mitch had spent $500 on a short-wave radio, so he could listen to the League on the World Service. With California eight hours ahead, he'd get up at six on Saturday mornings; the three-hour broadcasts started at six-thirty his time, with the games kicking off at seven. He'd cook himself his once-a-week treat, a full-on English breakfast – bacon, egg, tomato, sausage, beans and mushrooms, the works – then he'd listen to England going about its Saturday business.

In the first half, he said, they tell you all the goals as they come in – 'so I'm sitting having breakfast in Oakland, listening to Carlisle go one up over Hartlepool. Lovely. Then in the second half, they go live to one particular game. So when they say, "Welcome to World Service listeners" – that's me out there. I love it. I was eleven,' he said, 'when we won in '66. I went out in the back garden, and I cried.'

Mitch was with three friends. One worked in a marina in Florida; the others, one of whom was Florida's brother (an engineer), were both from Storrington, near Worthing.

Florida told me, 'We're all frustrated footballers at the end of the day.' He'd tried out with Chelsea when he was fifteen, when he'd been captain of Sussex Schoolboys; he said, with a smile that had the disappointment still tucked inside it, 'I'm still waiting for the phone call'. Later, in 1972, he'd had a trial for England Under-18s, in Skegness – and until only recently, he'd carried on playing in Florida. He'd played there, he said, alongside Johan Neeskens, from Cruyff's 'total football' side.

The four of them had met in Monterrey during Mexico '86, and they'd kept in touch. And when they'd arrived there, they said – a year after Heysel – the local papers had been full of HOOLIGANS, ANIMALS, MURDERERS.

'But individually,' said the engineer, 'the people were charming – they'd pick you up and give you lifts to wherever you were going – they'd take you in their cars with their families. There was bonhomie everywhere, the Mexicanos were magic. I felt embarrassed, because I knew they'd never get treated that way in England – one gentleman did remind me of that, he'd been at Everton in '66, and said it was a right shambles – but they wanted to impress, they wanted to be welcoming, and we really *felt* welcomed.'

And I only wish I could say I felt equally welcome while I heard these stories. But I wasn't – because at seven o'clock after Russia–Romania, we went off together to my favourite food haunt, the Trattoria La Taverna, to get a meal before Italy played Austria at nine. And as we arrived there, it came out that I had a press pass. They already knew I was writing a book – but the press pass made them instantly disbelieve that.

Not seeing English tabloids every day, Florida and Radio

Mitch were less hostile. But the other two were deeply, aggressively suspicious. They clammed up; they wanted me out of their company right away. And they weren't stupid men – at thirty-five, Radio Mitch was the youngest of them, and they were straight and articulate. In vain I told them, the press pass just came with the job I was doing – I really was writing a book. It didn't matter – the loathing and mistrust was potent and absolute. I'll condense what they said as follows, and I hope they'll agree that the précis is fair:

'You listen, pal – England fans have been libelled and maligned *en bloc* for so long, by so many lying scumbags who wouldn't know the truth if it bit them on the leg, that if you think some bullshit about a book's going to make us say *one word* to you, then either you're not living in the real world, or your just *right out of order*.'

There was a story that in Monterrey, there was a man from the *Sun* going round with a brick tied up in a note that said the brick was from England. And he'd go into bars offering fans a couple of hundred quids' worth of pesos to put it through a shop window.

I'd heard that story – or variants of it – enough times to reckon there might be something in it. Now, from these men, it seemed unanswerable.

It was about the most depressing and hard-fought conversation I've ever had over a meal in my life. They did, in the end, tell me their stories – but the two from England were grudging to the last.

When we parted company one of them said, 'I hope your conscience is clear.'

And when a press pass has become the mark of Cain like that, what hope can there be for the press to tell the truth *even if it wants to*?

Italy were magnificent – but so was the Austrian keeper Klaus Lindenberger, resplendent in an outfit like a day-glo zebra crossing in a swimming pool.

So although Italy's play had such a flow and a pace to it, such grace and skill and invention, they still had this big problem – they couldn't score. In seven previous internationals they'd only got two goals – against Algeria, and Switzerland.

And you don't win the World Cup, if you don't score goals . . . ten times they missed, or hit the post, or hit Lindenberger. Carnevale forced two saves, and scooped a sitter over the top from a couple of yards; Ancelotti and Vialli both missed twice; Giannini, De Agostini, and Donadoni all saw chances go astray – and Donadoni was denied a clear penalty by the Brazilian referee.

With sixteen minutes left, Vicini sent on Salvatore Schillaci, the little Sicilian who plays his football at Juventus. It was his fourth cap. Four minutes later, Donadoni passed, Vialli crossed – and with his first touch of the game, Schillaci rose high to head it home.

Comes the hour, comes the man . . . Italy 1, Austria 0.

It was fine football – but I've have enjoyed it more if I hadn't been with men scared to open their mouths in case I stitched them up, in a bar perpetually circled by film crews and photographers.

And if the *carabinieri* hadn't been gathered and watching outside the place all evening, tooled up in big groups by their vans, blue lights flashing in the dark.

Next morning, the day before England played Ireland, I took the bus out to Pula; a kind man in a bar drove me the last few kilometres from there to the guarded gates of Is Molas. When I said I'd seen Argentina in Milan, he said of Maradona, 'He thinks he is king, so he opens his mouth too much. A great player, yes – but also a complete idiot.'

The England players had a row of eleven rooms to themselves, along the lower tier of one wing of Is Molas. They looked out across a dry lawn towards the pool, and the sea beyond. They sat on their little terraces, waiting to go to training.

Bryan Robson was doing a crossword, and was phased by the last clue. 'Six letters,' he said, 'a shrill violent woman.'

'Missus,' said Shilton.

'It's a shite crossword anyway.'

I told him, 'virago'. A helicopter roamed overhead.

Butcher watched it pass. 'Dollarville, isn't it – fucking Dollarville.' He'd just read my book – they sit and read book after book, Ludlum, Martin Cruz Smith, Sidney Sheldon, anything that'll pass away the days.

Butcher said, 'This is the worst time. Been waiting so long now – you just want it to start.' He was unshaven, and he said he'd stay that way, 'until we win or go out'.

Millichip wandered about in an Umbro shirt, shorts and sneakers; Kelly lay beached by the pool. In the foyer, Brian Scott showed his arms and said unhappily, 'I'm still white.' No poolside time for him.

Des Walker said he'd talk with me – but he wasn't too happy. 'I know you're not press – but when the book comes out, the press'll still pick it up.' Brian Clough's strictures hung round him and Stuart Pearce like a ring-fence.

But I'd already spent my time that morning with Bobby Robson, and now they had to leave for training – so Des stayed safe from the press anyhow.

Exclusive: Bobby Robson eats prunes and peaches for breakfast . . .

Robson said he'd told Don Howe the team that'd start against Ireland on Wednesday 6th, the day after the kickabout in Oristano. He said, 'You have to clear your head. You can't go around saying, is it this, or is it that?'

Was Oristano helpful?

'A bit. A fraction.'

Was Tunis helpful?

'You take a risk. You take a gamble wherever you play. Prior to the World Cup you know, if you have a sub-standard performance, you'll get done – papers'll go mad. And they don't worry about players, they rip you to pieces – then they want to come and smile, and talk to you. Would you do it? Honestly, would you do it? I'm not saying they're all bad, they're not, some write good stuff – David Lacey, I'd share a glass with him, I'd go anywhere with him. But the tabloids, the muck, the derogatory stuff . . .

'Look, it was hot in Tunisia, it was eighty-two degrees. We got off to a decent start, we made some chances – could have had two before they scored. Then we make the most unbelievable error, and we're severely punished for it. Quite extraordinary, 'cos the feller hit about a forty-yard shot – and you're now in a different game.

'And are you going to tell me Tunisia are nothing? Look at

Cameroon – I thought Argentina might win 1–0. But when they go ahead they become elevated, these fellers – like Egypt, if they score first, they can do you. They'll get confident, they'll get aggressive – it was only through bloody persevering that we nicked a draw. Well, we didn't nick it, if you look at our possession – Peter Shilton did nothing second half, saved one free-kick – but you can't get through. They know how to defend.'

And the Butcher incident?

'I didn't see it. All I know is we got a lot of free-kicks, and they hang into you, they grab you – and the referee won't give penalties. So you're waiting for a free kick, you know the run you're going to make, and they're baulking you, they're dragging you, they're holding you – so Butcher's just gone, "Geddaht the way" . . . and he's caught the feller. He hasn't butted him, have you seen where he's cut – he's just shook the feller off 'cos he's grabbing him. And then I took him off, 'cos he's booked for it – knowing Butcher, he could make one injudicious tackle, one long-legged tackle, and we're down to ten men. And then, I needed to look at Wright anyway.'

I asked if he was over-loyal to a player like Butcher. He said he didn't play him because he was loyal to him, he played him because he was the best. Look at Shilton . . . then, recalling how Shilton had been criticised over Uruguay's two goals, he went off against the papers again. 'They fuckin' murdered him. SHILTS WILTS, all that – and then they expect him to talk to them? We are human people. Take Butcher, you look at what he's done for us. In September, I thought he had a red shirt on when he came off that pitch – thought he was playing for Wales. So now it's eighty-two degrees, he looks a bit slow, he's got his name taken, he's took his shirt off – and they go WHACK. No fuckin' loyalty.'

I asked how he answered the criticism that England were predictable.

'By results. We play the same way as Liverpool – we play the same way as Jackie Charlton. Jackie Charlton plays 4–4–2, he kicks the ball long – I don't see any criticism there. He's got results. Me, I've lost one in nineteen. Before the European Championships we lost one in sixteen, played everywhere – and I tell you what, when you're England, people want to beat you more than anybody else.'

So how did he feel, with thirty-six hours to go?

'Fine. I'm looking forward to it. I know the pressure I'm under, I've been through it before. I won't crack. Christ, if I couldn't cope I'd have cracked weeks and weeks ago, wouldn't I? Years ago. I just find it all sordid and bloody wicked, I really do . . . never mind.'

I wondered then, as we finished, having watched him work for nine months, whether there was ever any time when he wasn't thinking about football – about the next match, the next opponent, and the best team to tackle them.

'On the golf course. Or listening to music. I like the old evergreens, the old ballads – Ella Fitzgerald, Dionne Warwick, Shirley Bassey, Neil Diamond . . . love it. Or reading. I like James Michener, or Wilbur Smith. Robert Ludlum, James Higgins, stuff like that – I don't like the heavy highbrow stuff, can't take that. I like action. Who's that American guy . . . d'you ever see that picture with Humphrey Bogart where he's Captain Queeg, he's got the ball bearings in his hand – Herman Wouk. Brilliant . . . but otherwise – people think I'm drifting sometimes, but I'm just absorbed with it all really. I'm consumed with football, I have been for twenty years. Picking the team, training . . . people say I won't be able to retire. But,' he laughed, 'I think I will.'

I thought we were done then – but as we were about to get up and go back across the lawn he said, as if it was worrying him, 'I don't feel as though I've come out of this very well, talking about this press thing – but I just find it's a bit unfair, that's all . . . the players have conducted themselves ever so well. They're here to play the World Cup, and sometimes they want to keep out of it, keep out of the papers – I'm like that. I'm trying to keep out of the bloody papers, not get in 'em. But they want to see you all the time . . . the week with our wives, I thought it was a holiday – I never got a holiday.'

I asked in what way he thought he mightn't have come out of it well.

'Oh . . . by being a bit aggressive about it. But when I think what I've done over the last eight years . . . you should have seen them the other day. There's the English and the Italians together, and some Italian guy says, "Mr Robson, can you explain to me why it is, with your record, and the success of the England team, that your press are so critical of you?"

'I said, "You're asking the right question, but to the wrong person. You'll have to ask them."

'Silence. So I said, "They obviously didn't hear. Perhaps you'd like to ask it again."

'So the guy asks the same question. I said, "Good. Good question. You've asked the right question, but again, sir, to the wrong person. You have to ask them."

'*Not one replied*. They all sit there, heads down – not one stood up. Not one had any integrity to say anything to that question. And it just shows you what some of them are made of. I said, "There is your answer. We don't need to say any more." '

Then Millichip and Wiseman rolled past with a fat sheaf of newspapers. Wiseman said that Doug Ellis, the Aston Villa Chairman and Graham Taylor's boss, had written 'a lovely little article about the Chairman, that he's going to meet him on his yacht. "I'm going to invite Bert to settle the deal." ' The deal was, of course, compensation to Villa for Taylor moving into Robson's job.

'Forty bottles of champagne,' mumbled Millichip mysteriously in the background.

'So he's got about as much chance of us going on there as flying,' said Wiseman.

'Strike the deal before you go,' said Robson, 'then you can pop the champagne.'

Wiseman asked, 'Can you imagine what the council would say?' They descended into conspiratorial whispers, and bumbled away – happy old boys in their shorts in the sun.

Then Robson turned back to me and to the story of how no English journalist had stood up to that question. He said, 'I saw Bob Harris a bit later, and I said, "Your industry came out very well this morning." He didn't say anything.'

Harris was writing a book with Robson, a World Cup diary. They'd done the same together in Mexico – when I tried to get a copy from my library, they said there were two copies in the county. One in a prison, one in a youth custody centre . . .

Robson said, 'I still haven't answered that correctly, you know, about how I felt when we left. I felt dreadful.'

He was worried about being aggressive? He said, 'If this was a war, you'd shoot them.'

*

There's a story where it's raining, so Robson's with the press in one of the dressing rooms at the training field; and he's wanting to give Peter Went from the PA a real public bollocking for the rubbish story about his being booed when he watched Cagliari. But there's this woman at the back . . . Robson's got his temper restrained, while he tries uneasily and impatiently to find out who she is – and it turns out she's one of the journalists' wives. He wants her to leave, so he can get on and roast Went – but he doesn't quite know how to ask for this politely. Then anyhow someone tells him, it's raining outside. Robson snaps, 'Get her an umbrella.'

Typical of the man: he didn't want a woman in the room while he was swearing . . .

England trained on a little ground in Pula with one low stand, and a bare concrete wall all around. Opposite the locked gateway was a grubby dirt car park; milling about waiting in the sun and the dust were maybe a hundred press, photographers and TV, plus a fistful of fans, tanned and tattooed.

Barclay wondered aloud, 'What fiendish schemes are they hatching in there? England's legendary free-kicks . . . give it to Stuart Pearce, and close your eyes.'

I told the *Daily Mirror*'s Harry Harris how I'd had such a gruesome time with Radio Mitch's mates. He said, 'All right, but who's being stitched up? The fans? Or the guy who's getting his head sewn back together in the hospital? You ask England fans – they never start it, do they? Who does start a fight? At school, when it's one on one in the playground, who starts it? The kid who calls someone a four-eyed tosspot? Or the kid who punches him? That's hard enough – so how do you tell when there's a thousand of them?'

Fans always innocent, papers always guilty . . . the world isn't that simple.

Inside, Mike Kelly was firing shots at the three goalkeepers. Bull and Bryan Robson passed a ball idly back and forth in the middle, watched by Lineker – he'd said earlier, 'I'm doing nothing this morning. Noth-ing.' Gazza joined in with them, singing,

Every day, things are getting better
Going faster, like a rollercoaster

The others played a game in a tight area marked out with

little yellow plastic cones, different players taking turns in goal; they were limited to a couple of touches each, then pass, pass – the ball thudded off their boots as they called out to each other, Widdly, Widdly, Webby, Webby, Macca, Macca, – Webb belted a shot in, and Platt saved it in his gut, *oooph*. Webb grinned. 'Platty, you daft bastard.'

When they were done, they headed for the white bus with its splatter of logos. On their way, some talked a bit with pressmen here and there; others didn't, and walked straight past. Butcher talked to TV and radio, because 'tape can't lie'.

And he talked to the man from the *Star* – because he's got a contract that means he has to.

And a large hole gapes open in this I-hate-the-press scene.

Because whatever they said, they could never impose any press black-out *en bloc* – not when player after player was taking money from paper after paper, to talk 'exclusively'.

Bobby Robson does his diary with Bob Harris; and he's long been signed up for a few pieces a year in the *Mail on Sunday*. Then Waddle talks to the *Sun*, Lineker to the *News of the World* . . . and so it goes on.

In *The Glory Game*, his account of a season with Spurs in '71–'72, Hunter Davies tells a story of how he and four football writers are mistaken for Spurs players when they get off the plane in Nantes for a UEFA Cup game.

All four of the journalists in that story, nineteen years later, were still on the case in Sardinia.

Love 'em or hate 'em, these boys have been around. They have relationships with people in football, so that every player has a writer or two that he trusts – not necessarily from the paper he's taking money from, either. Bobby Robson, for example, said Steve Curry of the *Express* was a friend of his.

So the England fans proclaim that they're all innocent; and the England squad strike that aggrieved and harried tone of men perpetually misused . . . the world isn't that simple.

On the eve of England's first game, the fans, the players, the press – together we were tipping over into the broiling and fevered air of Planet Football, where the antagonism's veined through with unseen friendships and deals . . . back in

Florence, Gordon Taylor, the intelligent and likeable Chairman of the Professional Footballers' Association, would laugh with me or John Williams or Rogan Taylor about what an amazingly difficult man Brian Glanville could be.

Then he'd have dinner with him for three hours.

'Because,' said John Williams, 'they're all in the club together, aren't they?'

Wherever football goes, they all go too – the players, the writers, the administrators. They jockey and they bicker, like politicians or businessmen in any other large but essentially enclosed corporate entity.

And the flipside of their fraction and friction is, always, an unsplittable symbiosis.

They need each other.

'It's bollocks, this getting wiser as you get older thing. You might maybe get better at pulling birds but otherwise, you know – if you're not mature when you're fifteen, when will you be?'

'Who was it said life's a bowl of cherries? Wittgenstein?'

'Nah – it was Terry Downes. He goes up to the pianist and he says, "Can you play life's a bowl of cherries in 5/4 time?" And the pianist says, "Surely you mean 4/4?" "Nah," says Terry. "Life's – a bowl – of fuck – in' cherries . . ." '

We were headed back up the road to Stalag Forte, the luxury beachside press cage – me, Barclay, two others. 'In Argentina in '78,' says Barclay, 'there was this mangy cur that used to drag round the dustbins looking for scraps, out by the training field Scotland were using. And as Scotland's fortunes lurched from disaster to apocalypse (defeated by Peru, drawn with Iran, Willie Johnston sent home after failing a dope test) Ally MacLeod came over to do his conference one day, and he's pale and drawn – and he pats the mongrel and he says, "Ah well, least this little feller loves me." And the dog bites him.'

They recalled an article about MacLeod that began with the famous four-word para: 'Is the man mad?'

'Sitting on the fence a bit, that was.'

Barclay said it was his fourth World Cup, and he still loved it – the only problem was having to write about it . . . and also that, being a Scot, he was no England fan. 'I think they're the most unattractive team in the tournament. Don't get me wrong, I like the English – when they've lost. Winning doesn't suit them. They're like the Germans – they don't wear prosperity well.'

His favourite tournament had been the European Championship in '84 – no British sides. The football was fantastic – and all the paper ever wanted was just a few hundred words.

Over lunch by the gleaming sea, amid throngs of fat Germans and windsurfers, we talked about Milan Seed Cap, and the amazing banality of other American questions they'd heard. A gridiron player was once asked before a Superbowl, 'If you were a tree, what sort of tree would you be?'

'Bobby Robson,' said David Lacey, 'would be a weeping willow. And Bryan Robson . . . Dutch elm.'

Michelle Lineker was there, slight and pretty and, like her husband, fluent and intelligent – the only player's wife to spend the tournament in Italy. She was friends with the violinist Nigel Kennedy's Californian girlfriend – she, and Kennedy, were with ITV in some unspecified capacity. The Linekers have no kids, so it wasn't a problem – and then, as one journalist said, they weren't short of a bob or two.

In Harry Harris's room, I watched the Czechs slaughter the USA 5–1 in Florence. The TV had thirty-six channels, including the BBC, and a German station; the 'room' was a small apartment. It had two double beds – one of them had been commandeered by Marcel, a Dutch journalist whose luggage had all gone astray in the bowels of the Italian airline system. He was now living off Harris's fruit bowl and canapé tray.

Up in Florence, the Czechs got lazy – they should have scored eight. An American journalist later told me, 'It was like watching a train wreck.'

I had a ticket for Italy–USA in four days' time. Jeff Powell wandered in from his room next door, and said after a while, 'Fuck me, they'll get twenty in Rome. They should play it in the Colosseum.' When an American got sent off he said, 'He's lucky, he's just missed out on the Italians. What sport does he play anyway?'

Harris dictated the back page lead for the next morning's *Mirror* down the phone, off the top of his head. He'd spent two hours doing a fifty-five para preview for the inside spread – a 'fly the flag' piece, asking for a restoration of English pride after the traumas of '88. In the office, he said, they'd added a few paras – and one said that in Germany, England were 'outfought, outmanouevred, outclassed'. That, said Harris, was too heavy – he'd changed it. We'd been outfought by the Irish, outmanouevred by the Dutch, outclassed by the Russions, but not all three all at once . . . they could be naughty, he said. On his Argentina–Cameroon byline, they'd put 'Harry Harris in Milan' when he was in Cagliari. 'It'll be caught out and end up in a column somewhere. Why couldn't they just put, "Harry Harris in Italy"?'

Now they needed a think piece for the back page. While he watched the game he casually intoned, 'Paul Gascoigne faces a World Cup baptism of fire tonight . . .'

Harris speculated in fluent tabloid-speak on how Charlton would send out the Irish to wind up Gascoigne. Some guy back in the office would whack a headline on it.

'How many paras is that? Another couple, OK – "There will be more familiar battles . . ." '

When the game was done – and the drinks drunk, and the valet persuaded to bring the *right* hired BMW to reception – I got a lift with Harris and Steve Curry back into Cagliari. And this is how they defended their trade.

Curry said, 'The difference between the sports press and the rotters (the news men) is that we're on semi-holiday – we enjoy ourselves, we like the football, and we like the people in it. And it's very sad that they don't like us any more. But over the last five years in particular, with the intensity of the circulation war . . . the trouble is, there's just too many men here. Each paper's had two men out here from two weeks before it's even started – and there's not enough material for them. So the No. 2's are exaggerating little things, just to get something in the paper. The No. 2's are top-spinners, their game's putting spin on to quotes – but it's only really in the eighties that the papers ever made this a two-man job at all.

'Then in the last five years, you've got the new breed of sports editor [as Barclay succinctly put it, 'Yobs']. They're more interested in the headline than the content – the *Sun* took a tiny Shilton injury and ran a huge scare that it could wreck England's chances. And it was bollocks – we all knew he'd be training the next day. But then Harry's editor rings up and says, why didn't you get that story? And Harry can say, because it's not true – but which one will the punter buy?'

When Robson's move to PSV came out, the *Sun* – the same paper that was telling the guilder-stained traitor to PSV OFF – stuck notes under his hotel door, offering money for his story. The first offer, Curry and Harris were sure, was six figures – and they went back with new notes, two or three times . . .

'The *Sun* are liars,' said Harris, 'proven, unashamed liars – making out Peter Shilton's at death's door when all he's done is knock a knee, that's nothing to them. And they invest an awful lot of money in trying to dig out the dirt – but that's their game.'

From the man whose own paper was about to run the Hostess Isabella story (however much he himself may have disliked it) calling the *Sun* liars was just a touch disingenuous . . .

Curry, while he thought Robson had behaved with great dignity, said, 'I have to say that the FA has no decent kind of PR, they're totally amateur – Glen and David, they're very nice men, but they've no grasp of our needs. If the FA were in any kind of competitive industry, they'd have been out of business years ago.'

As to how the players felt, he said that with the No. 2's all scuffling about trying to find something (as if the No. 1's were above all that) each stretch, each exaggeration, each lie – naturally, it got the players more and more antagonised. 'I personally haven't found it that bad. But they have been turned over, so they're very, very careful – and you really can't blame them. And the situation's deteriorated, just recently – though I'd say it's not as bad as '82, with Keegan. Players were hissing and spitting when they came into press conferences then.

'The thing is, you can't all the time be praising people, can you? People criticised Butcher in Tunis – but why? Because he did something unbefitting to an international player, is why. Now someone like Gary Stevens, I can understand it, he's taken a pounding, including from me – I've given him unrelenting stick. But our players are more sensitive than others – when things are going badly, the Italian press can be far more vicious than we'll ever be. They crucify their players.

'Also, when players are criticised, they moan about it – but they sing like budgies when they're being paid.'

Then he said that actually, players fifteen years ago used to behave far worse than they do now, getting pissed, getting laid – 'There was a certain international goalkeeper, after a big night in Europe, we all got on the coach for the airport the morning after, and unbeknown to us, he's only just arrived back in the hotel and gone to bed. So we called from the airport and they put him in a taxi, and he's totally slaughtered. There's some car up on a dais on the concourse, and he's sitting in it, singing away at the top of his voice – an absolute embarrassment.

'But back then we misbehaved with them, they misbehaved with us, and there was an area of trust – it didn't get written. Those were the days, when we used to stay over Wednesday nights . . . and with the rotters now, that's all gone.'

Those were the days . . . when merry bands of Brits bonked and boozed their way round Europe, and not a soul ever to chide them.

Ever since Poland, I'd thought two things about the press. Firstly it wasn't, in the end, that they were bad people – it was, simply, that they were boys.

The players had got the best job, the job every boy dreams of, the job that lets you stay a boy for ever and be a hero too – but there's nothing heroic about writing. The writers couldn't play, so they got the second best job – and sure, it was a job any bright, cocky boy back at school would have been eager to get – but then they found it meant cursing your way down the aisle of a plane in the arse-end of Silesia at midnight, while the heroes drank champagne on the other side of the curtain . . . and it was all just harder and nastier than anyone ever told you. You went from city to city, stadium to stadium, bar to bar, season after season, with the yobs in the office on your back every day, demanding you write shit you knew was shit even as the words hit the screens of your lap-tops – and like any other teenage boy you got confused, you lashed out, you had great unreasonable drinking jags . . .

So football may well be, like politics or business, a great and amorphous transnational corporate entity, with its many different workers bitching and jockeying for kudos and position.

But with this big difference: it's an entity *populated by boys.*

And there's the tragedy of sport: that the boys have their dream – but the boys get older. And for every boy who doesn't get to the heart of it, playing on the field – for every boy not graced with the luck and the legs to live out the dream for real – for every boy bar those, the dream becomes a snare.

Football's a woman you can't leave (they say in Argentina, you can change your wife – but your club and your mother, never). So you may well fall out of love with it – but you've still got the mortgage round your neck, and another bloody game come Saturday to write about.

> *The burly striker soared above the heads of the despairing defence to head home unerringly.*
>
> *The silky skills of the subtle Latins left the Saxon yeomen lumbering.*

Hell – *I'd* drink . . .

Then there was this second thing I'd thought about the press, more and more since Poland – and it was a question not just about them, but a question that goes wider, to all of us: namely, in what way were they different to the hooligans? Looking back, as they do, to their youthful golden age of Euro-wide liquor and nookie . . . because for sure, they drink in better bars, and they don't smash them up afterwards. But they still drink – they drink, some of them, enough booze to float a battleship. And then, a lot more rarely, they fuck – just like English fans, or English tourists, or English businessmen, on packages on Corfu or the Costa Brava, at trade fairs in Hamburg or Houston, on sex safaris in Mombasa or Bangkok . . . just like Englishmen in general.

The hooligan is not some animal apart. He is our own logical conclusion.

He is us, all played out.

This is how RAMPAGE begins . . .

I went to the Bar Svizzera to watch Brazil play Sweden – and as a man in Kansas once asked me, did you ever see sardines in a can?

The place was packed with English, Irish, and Sard, all having a party time drinking together, and enjoying the game. It was noisy, it was cheerful – and it got photographers and TV crews like shit gets flies. People drank bottles of wine – way cheaper than beer – and they drank bottle after bottle, singing happily *Que sera sera*, England England, Cameroon Cameroon, You'll never walk alone, Cockles and mussels alive, alive-oh – and in honour of their hosts, they also chanted,

> *CA-LYAH-REE! CA-LYAH-REE!*
> *EE-TAL-YAH! EE-TAL-YAH!*

Best of all they sang, in unison,

> *We – all – agree*
> *England and Ireland are magic*
> *Are magic*
> *Are magic*

The hostility level was zero; the Brazil–Sweden game was wonderful. At half-time, Brazil were a goal up . . . but it was becoming impossible to see or hear any of it – and the little old lady who ran the place was getting scared.

I don't know if she called them, or if they came of their own accord – but outside, the baton merchants were gathering by the vanload.

And the trouble with the fans is, they can't see the end of a good thing. Several of us – one or two Irish, me, Radio Mitch – tried to tell people the *carabinieri* were with us and looking mean, and cooling the noise down would be a seriously wise move. But (with justice, after all) several replied that they were doing no wrong – while others were simply too boisterously drunk, too high on being together in a sing-song gang and, basically, too dumb, to know how or when to calm it down. The smarter and the more sober – the likes of Mitch and his mates – saw the danger, and began to leave. It only takes one glass . . .

Then the scum arrived – with a whole train of press in tow who'd been following them from bar to bar, just waiting for them to get things started – and giving them, of course, the global audience they crave. There were only four or five of them; they got up on to tables with their crewcuts and their piggy little eyes, and they barked out their poison, and their 'No Surrender to the IRA.'

It was wholly out of character with a loud but harmless evening, and it soured it utterly. They turned on the ice cream machine – brave boys – and green and white slop started spreading over the marble floor.

The regular fans, even the drunk ones, wanted none of this crap – more people began to leave. Others were still singing – though interestingly, when someone told the venom-heads that the police were on the brink of coming in, they hopped off their tables and – so courageous – fell silent immediately.

And, this time, it didn't go off. There was no RAMPAGE. But it had been only an inch away . . . and if it had gone off, a lot of people who did no wrong would have had their heads whacked hard, and their pictures in the papers.

There was, however, this great encouragement. You couldn't get the fans to pack it in because the police were there – but a good number of them packed it in for themselves anyway, when the ugly crew came, and walked away.

Out on the pavement among the swarming media, I found Colin Moynihan's press secretary. I believe – I hope – that he would have seen it that way too; and the next morning he did stress, at a conference for the rotters, that any trouble so far had been exceedingly minor, compared to the numbers of English in town.

Disappointed, the scum moved on with their eager retinue, and went looking for someone else to wind up. The old lady and her friendly waiters started mopping up the aftermath. With relief, no doubt, but also with genuine kindness, she said goodbye and goodnight to all the boys as they left. Several among them gave her little presents, English and Irish favours, green wool bracelets and a three lions pennant; while others charmed and flustered her, by giving her great boozy bear-hugs to say thank you – a strange and pleasant cross-cultural sight, these large and plastered boys in their ragged shorts and torn T-shirts, picking up and embracing this amazed, embarrassed, and rather delighted old Sardinian sweetie. And others shook her and the waiters by the hand – friends were made here, and it was *grazie* all round.

So I didn't see too much of it – but while we were narrowly avoiding RAMPAGE, Brazil beat Sweden 2–1; Maradona's Napoli team-mate Careca scored both the goals.

More ominously, the Germans stuffed the skilled and fancied Yugoslavs 4–1 in Milan. Captain Lothar Matthäus scored two screamers, and played Dragan Stojkovic off the park; while his Inter Milan colleague Jürgen Klinsmann put away a spectacular diving header. Together that night, Careca, Klinsmann, Matthäus and Rudi Völler all served notice that – though the Italians might have trouble scoring – there were Italian-based Germans and Brazilians who knew very well where the net was.

Meanwhile, German fans had a bit of a rampage of their own, smashing windows and looting for four hours through the city centre . . . two were jailed for a year, for attacking a policeman; forty-three were deported. And word came in of a new phenomenon: *East* German hooligans.

It's a common European home, boys.

I went back across Largo Carlo Felice to La Perla, got up to my room – and then the sirens went off, and a roaring of engines, and a screeching of brakes. Beneath my balcony a ragged group of English and Irish fled the flashing lights and the racing police vans out on Carlo Felice – then they span and hared back the other way, as a knot of Italian boys came pelting towards them, and spilling out across the main road. I legged it down the stairs and got outside, and found a pair of Irish, breathless and alarmed at the end of the sidestreet. One said, 'I'll tell you two things. I'm glad as hell I'm out of here to Palermo come Tuesday. And you wear an Irish shirt these next two weeks, feller – 'cos they're picking up anybody English out there just for nothing. For nothing.'

Hank appeared round the corner then with Duncan, an English boy who was also at La Perla – they were sweating and breathing fast, and absolutely scared shitless.

They said they'd been coming off a sidestreet at the top of the Largo to come down to the *pensione*, and they saw three English boys walking across a zebra crossing – doing nothing at all, just crossing the road – and suddenly an unmarked white Fiat with its lights off comes streaking up the hill; narrowly it misses these three boys, as it screeches spinning to a halt. Then out jump three plainclothes men; two of them grab one English guy, the other two run.

'And the third police guy,' says Hank, 'he goes down in a crouch like it's fucking Los Angeles – and he's got a fucking gun. He's waving a fucking gun about. And he's shouting in Italian to the other two to stop – but what use is that?'

Meantime, the other two agents are pistol-whipping the one they've grabbed on to the back seat of the car.

So now being English on a zebra crossing is an offence to be dealt with by handgun?

Out on the Via Roma, Italians and English were making little runs at each other – *fuggi fuggi*, nothing serious. And the police were even whacking the photographers . . . Duncan said he saw one English lad on the floor with a bloodied face.

Then he said that since four in the afternoon (and this was confirmed by fans all over Cagliari the next day) there'd been press and TV from every country in Europe buying drinks for the boys all round town.

No arrests; one boy hospitalised for the night.

And like Harry Harris said – just who *does* start all this?

The BBC's Rob Bonnet filed material suggesting that the police were being insensitive and provocative.

Even the *News of the World* talked about 'bloodthirsty Italian police' – but then, the tabloid agenda had an interesting spin on it.

Moynihan's press secretary said one radio report about the *fuggi fuggi* had been so over the top, it had been brought up at a Downing Street briefing – where people were told that this exaggeration didn't help. This was not, of course, what they'd been told after Stockholm – but now it was be-nice-to-football time, and the government was saying we don't want RAMPAGE any more . . . so the tabloids started laying into the Italians instead.

PASTA JOKE

The Italians had 7,000 police and *carabinieri* on Sardinia – more police than there were England fans . . . '90 Tour had sold less than half of their 3,000 packages; with the FA selling most of their allocation of 2,816 tickets, and then a few hundred buying in the street, I'd say the Irish outnumbered the English in the Sant'Elia by two to one at the very least.

A pathetic cretin called Chris Wright – 'the man in the top hat' – went about in his ghastly crimson and sky-blue Crystal Palace gear, telling people there'd be a march on the stadium from the rail station at six. With abominable irresponsibility, he told people if they turned up that way without tickets, they'd get in . . . fat chance.

The stadium was an armed camp. Hundreds and hundreds of police and military were ranged all around it, with rifles and handguns; there were mounted police, and police with dogs, and a pair of helicopters circling above. Round the back of the ground, dozens and dozens of dark blue police buses and vans stood empty in rank after rank in the parking lot, and spilled over in a long line along the sealed-off overpass where the main road went by. I thought, who's worried about Abdul Needle? The force was so heavy, Saddam Hussein would have thought twice.

By the quickest way, the stadium was a half-hour walk from the centre of town – but you couldn't go the quickest way. You had instead to go north-east along Viale Armando Diaz, beyond the stadium, and then cut back and come down to it from the far side. I really don't know what the point of that was, especially as it took you through shops and houses –

whereas the quickest way went under the main road by the south side of the industrial estate, well away from any breakable property. But then, like the Light Brigade, it's not the football fan's lot to reason why . . .

Along the way, locals sold wine out of car boots. Drinks ban? Ha – some of the boys who'd been on my plane turned up from their campsite that morning, in a van loaded with crates of beer they'd bought the day before . . . but it did work overall. Along the Via Roma all day, fans sat subdued in front of mineral water and Coke – a sorry and rather comical sight.

When they got to the stadium, they were searched and searched again. All their coins were taken off them, and you can understand why – but you can't call it fair that they didn't get them back. And people lost all kinds of other stuff, in this draconian shake-down – shaving foam, toothpaste, even plastic mineral water bottles were confiscated when, arriving three hours before the game, it was hot in there. But that was too bad – get out your notes, and buy the franchise man's sponsor-fizz instead. I saw one Irishman staring in disbelief, as a policeman frisked his green teddy bear.

Arriving in big bands, the Irish sang,

Oooo – laaaay . . . o-lay, o-lay, o-lay

And the English march arrived from the station, singing 'God Save the Queen'.

I got into the press centre at 5.25, twenty-five minutes into Scotland's game in Genoa against the perky Costa Ricans. Hugh McIlvanney sat in torment before the TV by the bar; he said, 'They're fucking hopeless – just like we thought.' Then he pointed at Jeff Powell and said, 'Him and his lot'll be getting the sneers ready.'

Sure enough, the English journalists were grinning fit to burst. When I asked how it was going, one said, creased up, 'Oh, they're holding out. Costa Rica have only had three or four chances.' And at half-time they said, 'Only forty-five minutes away from a point.'

In the fiftieth minute, one Juan Cayasso performed the four-yearly ritual of breaking Scottish hearts – a colleague's deft backheel set him free, and he scored from close range. At the other end, Luis Conejo acrobatically kept out what little the Scots could throw at him. McIlvanney jerked and jumped at each lost chance in his chair, his face a kaleidoscope of rage and despair over the wretched fate of having to follow his unbelievable team.

Costa Rica 1, Scotland 0. Or, as the *Guardian* splendidly put it:

SCOTLAND PLUNGED INTO CAYASSO

In Glasgow, the *Daily Record*'s headline said sadly:

STOP THE WORLD CUP, WE WANT TO GET OFF

The Costa Rican President moderately announced, 'This is driving us crazy with satisfaction.'

But there was worse to come yet from British football tonight.

The England team arrived two hours before kick-off with four outriders, and seven or eight cop cars all flashing their lights. The chopper that had attended on their passage joined the other two over the stadium; they buzzed and clattered close above our heads, drowning out the shuffle and whisper of fans' feet across the Tarmac. They walked in lines past the railings, and weaved through the staring gangs of weaponed and uniformed men. The green of Ireland was everywhere; they'd come in whole families, men and women and children, and they looked a happier lot altogether.

But then, if they lost they'd not cry over it; whereas if England lost again as they'd done in '88, with the Dutch still to come . . . that was *unthinkable*.

Clouds sat along the ridge-tops of the far hills across the bay; the hills stood in a gorgeous hazy rank of grey-blue silhouettes against the last, soft-edged evening light. I turned and went up into the wide bowl of the Sant'Elia.

With half an hour to go, the Curva Nord was all tricolours; the Curva Sud was Union Jacks, and the Cross of St George. The message that appears at sports events the world over was here too: 'John 3:16'.

The verse reads, 'For God so loved the world that he gave his only Son, that whoever believes in him should not perish but have eternal life.'

The Irish had put their own private twist on it: 'Jack 3:16'.

The Union Jacks, meanwhile, announced Gravesend and Aston Villa, Poole Town and Hull City, Oldham and Wood Green . . . we are England. On poles opposite the press box flew the flags of the four nations in Group F, along with flags for Cagliari, Italy, and FIFA – the two spheres of the world on two footballs.

There were *carabinieri* with dogs and rifles all round the running track; others stood in big bunches round the upper rim of the top tier.

The new floodlights were bright under the darkening sky – it was now a rich indigo sheet, laced round the horizon with tufts of mauve and pink cloud. It was very breezy, too, and a little bit chill – a lot of the journalists were shivering in shirt sleeves. But not me – the excellent Signora Orru gave me weather reports every match day, for my £8.50 a night . . .

The teams came out, and the stands popped and crackled with flashlights. Oddly, the Irish turned to face away from the cameras across the pitch, when their anthem was played. A man from the *Sun* said, 'Not many of them know the words.' This is a side, after all, whose Irishness is determined for the most part only by the odd grandparent here or there – there's a story of a new Anglo draftee joining the team on some foray into Europe, and the anthems get going, and he turns to the player beside him and says, 'Blimey, this one goes on a bit.'

And the other guy says, 'Shush – it's ours.'

Where do they come from, after all? Apart from the scouser John Aldridge playing at Real Sociedad in the Pays Basque, the Irish side starting in Cagliari had two Celtic players, two Liverpool, and two Aston Villa, with the rest coming from Millwall, Blackburn, Norwich, and Everton – so you want English football? Go watch Ireland.

When the sides were named, Stevie Bull – as a substitute – got the biggest English cheer; but the Irish names garnered far greater and more noisy support, and Jack Charlton the biggest roar of all. Can a crowd have an accent? Sure can:

OIRE-LAND! OIRE-LAND!

The Irish looked dangerous immediately, a long throw on the strong wind going right into the heart of the box; Shilton got crunched in a sandwich of green shirts. And sure enough, they were off and at it at 200 mph; Gascoigne got warned, as the tackles started flying. It was hassle, hassle – two men on Barnes every time he saw the ball, forcing error, shutting down space – not football, just mayhem, with the ball in the blowy air all the time, and no end of argy-bargy in the box.

Surely England had the class to overcome this dreck ... Bryan Robson headed a Gascoigne free-kick wide – Moran tumbled Lineker after a neat touch had him turned and left standing – then, on eight minutes, Waddle released an immaculate ball from the flank into the teeth of the wind, and into Lineker's sprinting path. He chested it past Bonner; Bonner tried to bring him down with a leg swung at his knees – but Lineker hurdled him and just kept to his feet, stabbing both himself and the ball all together into the net as two desperate Irishmen fell crashing on his back.

It was a brave and typical goal, wolfishly taken with electric pace – his thirty-second for England, in fifty-two games. And that's no mean record.

You're not singing
You're not singing
You're not singing any more

But the Irish shovelled back into it. Gascoigne was showing nice touches, playing smart passes round the middle; but Ireland defended in dense numbers, and pressed and pressed without cease – they kept on sticking two men to Barnes to cancel him out, and they bundled Lineker and Beardsley around without compunction.

In the wind it was awkward; the German referee kept interfering – and the brutish hullaballoo didn't give him much choice. The wind grew stronger; a shivering journalist joked, 'I always knew it'd be a difficult contest for the Irish in this heat.' Getting bored, the English sang,

We won't pay no poll tax
We won't pay no poll tax
La la la la
La la la la

After twenty-five minutes, an alarming incident: chasing yet another long ball, Aldridge and Des Walker tussled and fell together over the goal line, and Walker crashed into the advertising hoardings. He played on, but for the rest of the game he was limping – and Des Walker with an ankle sprain was bad news indeed, with the likes of Van Basten lurking down the road.

Meantime, every Irishman who got the ball, you could tell what he was thinking like he was shouting it through a megaphone: 'How high and far can I kick the thing this time?' Floodlight height . . . things got scrappier and scrappier, England sinking with their opponents to the Wimbledon level. And always there was the vague and unlikely fear that they'd lose a goal, as the Irish kept hoofing it at random into the box. They didn't make chances, they just caused confusion – but that kept Shilton more busy than Bonner ever was. Butcher, I noticed, yawning, as he headed away another moonshot, had shaved after all.

The thing degenerated into abject chaos. Either the ball ricocheted about like it was pinball, not football; or some rare and brief interruption that threatened English quality was abruptly terminated by another train crash of a tackle. Barnes was invisible – his first look of something like a real run wasn't until nearly forty minutes had gone by. He was, of course, sent arse-over-tip, and the free-kick led to a chance; but it was the first clear thing that had happened in ages. At half-time we watched our monitors, wondering grimly what RAI TV might do for highlights – because the goal apart, there hadn't been any.

I went out the back of the stand to go down to the press centre for a coffee – and there, rushing towards us across the Gulf of Angels, was a vast and spectacular electrical storm. Huge streaks and ructions of lightning flew from fierce black clouds all round the bay.

It hit us just as the second half began, and the rain came sheeting down . . . so much for acclimatisation. We might as well have been on Merseyside, or Tyneside.

The postage stamp roof over the press box didn't cover all the out-lying positions; we scuttled for shelter, as monitors fused and died all around us, and sat grousing in a huddle at this continuing worthless jungle of a game. It picked up where it had left off – except now the turf and the ball were wet, and the play was even worse.

Only Gascoigne really stood out now and then, sharp and light in the middle of things; Barnes had disappeared completely. I sat hunkered on my haunches behind a pair of demented Colombian radio commentators talking nineteen thousand to the dozen – God knows what about, it can't have been the game, the game was a dog. Maybe they were letting the folks back home in Barranquilla know in Cagliari they have tropical storms too – they were an amphetamine double act. The lightning raced past over our heads, truly Spielbergian in its scope and drama.

Then, on the hour, Waddle set off from deep in his own half. He skipped past one man, cut in, left another man standing, and got into the area – so Moran simply toppled him. It was a hack to the ankles as obvious as if he'd brought him down with a baseball bat.

Bobby Robson said later it was 'clear as day'.

But we don't get penalties, do we?

In the sixty-ninth minute, Robson took off Beardsley, and sent on Steve McMahon to bolster the midfield – which you might say was sensible enough, in the dismal chaos out there, because he wanted to be sure and hold the lead.

Instead, he lost it. McMahon had been on for four minutes when, with only his third touch of the ball, he lost control of it on the edge of the box. It bobbled off his right foot – Kevin Sheedy pounced, and fired it in first time.

In the next minute, an inch-perfect Gascoigne free-kick, a lovely curling ball, went just a bare yard wide from Butcher's head. And on eighty minutes, a Barnes chip across the box passed a hair's breadth away from Lineker's brave dive.

And that was the sum total of England's riposte. Robson sent on Bull for Lineker with six minutes left – but by then, we were in a ruin of bewilderment.

The tortured McMahon saw red, tangled with McGrath, and got booked.

A minute or two later, Gazza damn near did the same – he came within inches of punching Chris Morris's lights out. But, mercifully, he remembered where he was just in time – turned the wrestle into a hug and a handshake.

And you could say, with hindsight, that that moment of self-collection – on the brink of disaster – was a turning point on the road to maturity for one of the greatest players of Italia '90.

But it didn't look that way then, not on 11 June. It looked, playing the way we were, like we'd get tonked by the Dutch, and in all probability by the Egyptians too. It looked like we'd be coming home in no time, in anguish and in bitterness, to the sound of a howling deluge of recrimination and fury.

Meanwhile the Irish fans went spare, and fair enough:

We're on the march with Jackie's army
We're all going to Italy

The English were silent – misery in the rain.

My soaked monitor had, mysteriously, retrieved a one-inch-wide strip of the picture – it was like watching the game through a fence.

But it had never been worth even squinting at.

England 1, Ireland 1.

ENGLAND IN A SHAMBLES

BOBBY'S BUNGLERS

ARTLESS, CHARMLESS, WORTHLESS

They were absolutely right – it was an abominable display. And yet to be honest, looking at the papers now, the English press if anything were almost tolerant of their team's witless scuffling.

Following Robson's cue, they pointed out that though we may have failed to counter it, we did still all know what the Irish would be like. In Jack Charlton's reign the Irish, after all, had been beaten only five times in thirty-eight. Robson told people to hold the criticism until they'd seen whether the Dutch fared any better against the 'biff-bang' long ball.

And David Lacey wrote in the *Guardian*, 'When it is the Egyptians' turn, they may think back nostalgically to the days when all that afflicted them from the heavens were frogs.'

But blaming the Irish was no excuse. It wasn't just that the football had been awful – but that the whole English approach had seemed gutless. It's all very well saying how stoutly we defended – and, we did, we fought, messy and ugly and tedious though that was – but with the likes of Barnes and Waddle on the park, what the hell were we doing defending all the time in the first place?

When Lineker got the ball, as often as not he was on his own up there – the midfield just sat back and held. But there was no such chickenshit hesitation from the Irish. Sure, they put every man and his dog behind the ball when they didn't have it; but when they did have it, and they pumped it up via the nearest passing stormcloud in the general direction of Tony Cascarino, what did they do then?

They surged up to join him and help out.

I think the problem was this. Bobby Robson had said to me, 'I know the pressure I'm under, I've been through it before' . . . and he was, as we know, a conservative man, with a horror of England losing, and an acute awareness of the rage that would be vented on his head if we did lose. So I think he sent his team into a game that he knew would be a scrap *promoting* caution. And Macca and Gazza would, in effect, say as much the next day.

So what happened? We played cautiously – we played downright badly – and the Irish made the running. Then Robson made a cautious substitution, the substitute made a mistake, and Sheedy said thanks very much and got a draw.

Robson said it would be a different business when it came to playing the Dutch – he said we could play some football then. But on the evidence of the Ireland game, there was little comfort in that. The mind went back to Germany '88, and the devastating Van Basten scoring three times in twenty minutes . . . *that* was football.

And here at Italia '90, we'd had twenty-one goals from the first eight games – we'd had Italy, Brazil, West Germany, Romania, the Czechs and Cameroon, all looking in their different ways like rampant class acts – *that* was football.

Whereas England–Ireland, the first draw of the tournament, had been nothing better than an oafish mêlée.

Dejected, I went to have a look at what the rest of the world was up to; I keyed in the Italia '90 News section of the Databank. But there was no news.

A steward said, 'The news is broken.'

Some time after midnight, I went back into town with Matthew Engel from the *Guardian*. We found the blue lights flashing, the vans all massing – the predictable malarkey.

We parked on the Via Roma. A bunch of English were gathered ahead of us at the main entrance to the station; as we crossed the foot of Largo Carlo Felice, a scattering run of *ragazzi* came our way, and then broke up. We backed off a minute; and then went on again.

But nothing much was happening. There was just, instead, this simple problem, which the FSA, the FA, and the embassy had all told the Cagliari police and *comune* would arise, and which had now arisen – because no one in Cagliari had listened.

With games starting at nine in the evening, all public transport had packed up long before the fans were let out of the stadium. But a fair few of England's supporters were staying on campsites out at places like Pula, thirty or more kilometres away – so how on earth were they going to get there? A cab was thirty quid, minimum – so these drenched and discombobulated boys were now marooned as well.

Glen Kirton said the next day, 'We said to them in September, you must put on public transport. We said to them in December, you must put on public transport. We said to them in February, March, April, and May, you must put on public transport. We spoke to them last week and said, you must put on public transport. I sent a fax to the COL two days ago saying, we have been attempting for a long period to get public transport put on to take the fans away from the game – we're getting no response – can you use any influence with the powers that be in Cagliari, to try and get this done? So on this issue it's absolutely not a case of the FA doing nothing – just nil response from the people who could effect it locally.'

Yet they could handle laying on extra ferries to ship the Irish off overnight to Palermo – so why not a few buses to get the English down the road?

The authorities later claimed that, in fact, they had laid on buses – but that at half-time they'd *forgotten to announce it* . . . PASTA JOKE indeed.

Things would be nastier later, come Turin. But on top of the transport foul-up, this was also an early occasion where the intimidating armed presence that encircled the English now offered protection, as well as threat – because one or two local lads fancied testing their mettle on the famed hooligans now gathered so conveniently . . . there was word of one of them swinging a bike chain about.

The minority of English who wanted to make something of it made a surge or two – hence the scatter of *ragazzi* as we arrived.

And the majority who didn't want to mix it (though bear in mind that they were sober here, which definitely did help) – they were backed into the station concourse, with a cold and uncomfortable night ahead.

The *carabinieri* inserted their considerable, riot-ready numbers, and drove off the Sard boys with a surge or two of their own . . . and then we all just stood there.

So what next?

The official Sant'Elia attendance that night had been over 35,000 – not a full house, but not bad – and the game had produced the stadium's all-time record takings, over £1,000,000. And where did the money go? There were twenty-seven officially supplied Cromas and Tipos and Unos and Pandas smoothly ferrying the bigwigs about – but what was there for these boys?

They'd travelled far, and, many of them, paid over the odds into those takings of £1,000,000 via the sharp hands of touts – and yet now, there was nothing, not even a bus home. Just a station platform to sleep on, because their tents were too many miles down the road . . . it was a scene right out of the English game: the money ploughing back into the pockets of the fat cats at the top – and to hell with the punter at the bottom.

And the only people I saw there, actually there on the ground, trying to do anything for them, were Craig Brewin, and Steve Beauchampe, and John Tummin of the FSA . . . someone said Moynihan was there – but where? Doing what? Reading police reports?

And Doug Ellis was there, and David Dein the chairman of Arsenal, and Jarvis Astaire of Wembley Stadium Ltd., merrily confabbing on yachts offshore – while the people who paid their wages sat wet and tired in the small hours on a cold marble floor; or stood and watched the blue lights flashing all around them, and the *carabinieri* hefting their guns.

Kirton said next day, it wasn't true that the FSA were the only people on the ground. The FA had their office in town, they had two security officers out at midnight the last three nights, they had undercover police . . . but these people needed help, not surveillance.

At one point a group of Irish were marched in to join the English. 'For their own safety,' someone said – but the Italians applauded them as they passed.

Engel sighed, 'I don't think the police quite understand the nuances here.'

Then someone said that buses were coming. Beauchampe sighed, 'Yeah – they're just building them now.' Then he added, with an unintentional but ghastly prescience, 'I suppose they'll have to crash a few on the way here first.'

Sometime towards two in the morning, buses did finally come, and the weary boys loaded up to get back to their campsites.

That still left maybe 150 to sleep in the station. The platforms and the ticket hall looked like the underground in the Blitz. A bright or lucky few had sleeping bags; others simply lay on the floor, some wrapped in their flags. It wasn't a good night for it.

As I left, I passed one fan articulately berating a high-up plainclothes man in the back of an unmarked car. He said, 'Look, this isn't our fault. There's no cheap rooms here, and no transport – what do you *expect* us to do?'

But the guy only slammed his door, and drove off.

Matthew Engel wrote in the *Guardian*, 'It is not easy finding sympathy for football fans. You cannot blame the Sardinians for being careful; Britain is the only country which sends a government minister round telling other countries how dreadful his fellow citizens are.

'But there is in this the same kind of thinking that precipitated Hillsborough. Obsessed by security, the authorities here have apparently given minimal thought to the simple logistics of moving crowds in and out of the stadium and back to their billets. Or of providing suitable billets, be they ne'er so humble. The scene at the station was pathetic, in more ways than one.'

I asked Glen Kirton about this the next day. The FSA, I told him, was enjoying a rising reputation among the fans – while the FA was widely disliked. (I put it mildly.)

He said, 'I'm not surprised. But the people you're talking about, they're not by their very nature going to accept the FA as a body that has their interests at heart. And the FA, you have to accept, over a period of time, has had very good reason to consider these people as potential enemies of the game. I don't know how many of them would accept this – they believe that they're out there supporting England, and supporting football – but over the years, they've been the people who have actually brought football down. So after Heysel – not just Heysel, but after Luxembourg '77, after Denmark '79 – we've said, please don't go . . . but they still come. And they've become the focus of the press – by their very presence, they've become anti-football.'

But anti or pro, they're there – and they look at the FA and think, the FA's got money (annual turnover approx. £14,000,000), and the FA's making money here in Italy – yet all there is is two ticket desks in a backstreet hallway. And they've got to pay £10 on top of the ticket for a temporary Travel Club membership. Now you could say, They're not our responsibility . . .

'No, I'm not saying that. We're not saying that. We want the Travel Club to *be* a Travel Club – we want to start turning it into a club that gives benefits to the people who join, not just the people here, but the whole range of football supporters – we want to start offering them reasonable travel all across the board. Because if there's been any commercial exploitation here, you know where it's come from. It started with FIFA selling the rights to '90 Tour . . .'

Later, after the Egypt game, I had a word with Pat Smith, the FA's ticket manager. She said tartly of the FSA that of course supporters had a role – but how did I think she came to have her job? Because, of course, she was a fan herself – she'd been a fan since she was eleven.

But she also said that they'd been in daily contact with the FSA – four, five, six times a day. She said they served a need, and that the FA recognised that they did.

And she said it was all very well, the FSA saying the football embassy was the first thing of its kind – but the FA's office was the first time they'd tried it too.

She rejected the accusation I'd heard from fans, that the £10 Travel Club fee was just the fans being made to pay for an under-the-counter ID scheme. It was, she said, £5 to join, and a £5 annual subscription – it was the only way they could organise the ticketing, which didn't come cheap. And, she said, they'd been working in their office since 6 June from 8.30 in the mornings, often until 9 at night – taking half-hour lunches, sorting accommodation, taking one guy to hospital, taking another to a clinic for a rabies injection . . .

There are people at the FA who feel they are unjustly traduced by the fans. Watching them work in Cagliari – and however much they may have been bungling or complacent or inert in the past – it was easy to sympathise with that feeling. All the same – if, as Kirton said, some fans' attitude to the FA is now steeped way too deep in mistrust and hostility, then who else can reach them?

The FSA can.

So if both sides drop their wary postures, and their fearful suspicions over 'politics' – then co-operation could prove fruitful indeed.

Already, in Cagliari, the beginnings were there. The FA, as Bloomfield had said, might not glide into action – but the sounds of its clunking, in Cagliari, were positive. The offices of the two bodies were both firsts – underfunded and ill-prepared, maybe – but at least they were there.

And later, by the time we all got to Turin, the possibilities of co-operation were being recognised even more. So there's grounds for optimism here – because if Kelly & Co. can see it, I don't doubt Kirton & Co. can enact it.

On 11 June, the idea that England might end up in the World Cup semi-finals in Turin was, frankly, preposterous – after the way we'd played against Ireland, you had to question if we'd get to the mainland at all. British football, all round, was the laughing stock of the tournament.

Beneath Matthew Engel's report on the aftermath of England–Ireland on 13 June, the *Guardian* ran a report from the Scottish camp at Rapallo. One of the Scottish players asked, 'Just one thing. Don't say we were as bad as England.'

The Scottish, having blown their best hope of two points against Costa Rica, were now preparing to play Sweden – who had, after all, given Brazil a fair run for their money.

But the Scottish manager Andy Roxburgh said, 'The thing is, we know about Sweden. We know the sort of game they play. It will be more like a typical British match.'

To which the response of the *Guardian*'s man in Rapallo was:

'Those who had watched the England–Ireland game drew hands over eyes and shuddered.'

The local papers next morning said that there'd been no incidents, and sport had been the winner – in theory, at least.

GREAT PARTY, AWFUL GAME

Outside the Bar Svizzera I met a scaffolder from Wimbledon, and a carpenter and a steel erector from Wolverhampton, all heavily tattoed. Also with them was the guy who sold fire protection equipment, who'd been on Stockholm's SHIP OF SHAME – and then a fifth bloke, a Chelsea man. When I asked him what he did he said, 'I dunno what you'd call my job.'

'Fuckin' scrounger,' said a Wolves boy.

He said, 'I work for this very rich person, I sell things for him – antiques, mostly . . .'

One of the Wolves lads said, 'That's gonna look good in his book, innit? Been goin' round with this guy these last couple of days, and now it turns out he's a fuckin' fence.'

These boys had got into Cagliari station from Olbia late on Sunday – the night when there'd been minor *fuggi fuggi* up and down the Via Roma – while the Brazilians and the Germans were winning up north. And in that rumpus one local kid, thirteen years old, had got his leg cut by glass shrapnel from a flying bottle – so now, said these guys, when they turned up, 'There were hundreds of Italians out there, baying for blood. I wanted to get right back on that train, I tell you. And the police were ready just to let us walk straight into it – no way. No fuckin' way.'

They said, with admiration and gratitude, 'Some bloke from the FSA got us out of there – got one of his rear windows smashed doing it – but he got us out, and he drove us to Sarroch.' They would, they said, have been 'ironed out' otherwise.

But mostly, they said, the Sards seemed great. In Sarroch they'd found a bar, and the guy who ran it, 'He was brilliant. We've known him two hours, and he lets us sleep on his floor.

Then yesterday in the morning he makes us coffee, and gives us a lift back into town – and he looks after our bags at his place, while we're here at the match. Brilliant.'

A little girl came by begging, and they all gave her money. One said, 'Aw, 'kin 'ell . . . it's only a kid. Bet she thinks it's her birthday.'

And they asked, 'How come the Irish can get a drink, and we can't? We had great crack with the Irish at the game last night – I've not met a bad one.'

But another said, 'They're not perfect. There was twenty at the top here, yesterday afternoon, grouped up and singing IRA stuff. And there was eight of us, we picked up our Union Jacks and walked away, I can't be doing with it. 'Cos I was in the ATC, see, me and five mates at home – and four joined, but not me, I got a job as a butcher. So then two of the four got killed in Ulster – land mine.'

There's good reason, after all, why some people – like Terry Butcher – can't be doing with rebel songs.

I had an idea how awful Steve McMahon must be feeling. Never mind that the football had been dreck – on any other day he could have gone on for those last twenty minutes, he could have held the midfield solid, he could have played the kind of hustling blinder he turns in for Liverpool every Saturday – and then the world would have been a different place altogether.

It would have been England 1, Ireland 0.

Steve McMahon is exactly the kind of English player that the Italians admire, the kind of player of whom Bryan Robson is the exemplar, the paragon – the type of player that the Italians describe, wistfully wishing they had such men themselves, as *duro*. But he'd gone out for his country in the World Cup – and had a nightmare.

I called him up and he said, yes, he'd talk about it.

So I went to the station, and waited for the next bus to Pula.

Outside the main entrance, a battered old taxi sat dented and bruised, and splattered with graffiti proudly announcing, 'Northampton – Old Car – Yes Yes Girls – Tourists Welcome – Very Old Car – Life Is Taxi'.

Life is taxi – but buses are budget.

So we rumbled along the road to Pula, and I read the Italian match reports as we went. They kept drumming it in: *una partita brutta*.

The bus passed through Sarroch, and climbed the slope beyond. Cagliari floated across the bay behind us, a creamy blur in the heat haze; between the vivid blue sea and the cloudless sky the town was a pale hillside jumble, shimmering through the flares of the refinery.

In Pula, a bunch of half-cut English lads got on, heading back for their campsite. They called out cheerfully, 'Drive on, Pedro!'

'Nah, cocker, wrong country. Spiros, innit. Drive on, Spiros!'

'Fuckin' berkhead – Luigi, innit, this is Luigiland. Drive on, Luigi!'

And when we set off:

Here we go, here we go, here we go

I got down at the turn-off into the broiling day. Insects buzzed and whirred as I walked the last couple of kilometres up the side road to Is Molas, and then bantered, gasping, with the police at the gate. They said they liked the English team, they were thoroughly *simpatico* – shame about their football . . .

Macca was waiting with Gascoigne in reception. I wondered if there was something instinctive about that – because when you need cheering up, there's no better boy for it than Paul Gascoigne. He can be genuinely funny, and he's wildly unpredictable – barking out his daft and irreverent comments, bouncing around, stillness quite beyond him – until there's nothing you can do but just watch him and laugh.

But behind the tomfoolery he can be, in his way, very sussed, even sensitive – because no doubt, since September, this boy was growing up.

So he was the right person for Steve McMahon to have about him on a day when you could tell, he was burning up inside so bad, it made the Sardinian sun look like ice. He showed us his chest – he'd torched himself, he was halfway between chocolate brown and brick-red.

I imagined him laying taut and miserable in the fierce glare, going over and over in his head how the ball had bobbed up off his foot – and then that last desperate lunge to retrieve it as Sheedy went round him, and fired it in.

He said the ball had been greasy, and the way it had come to him had been difficult to control; he'd only just gone on, he hadn't got his touch yet, and it was a thing could have happened to anyone . . . but it had happened to him, and boy, did he know it. The way he spoke about it had a pained and furious urgency, ill-restrained.

And it was pig-awful luck, too, to have made that mistake in front of millions the world over . . . but that's the World Cup, and Steve McMahon held his hands up. The fact was the fact; when we talked, he never ducked it.

We walked down to the golf club to get a beer; they readily agreed as we went, it had been a dreadful game. Macca asked Gazza, had he heard? – they were getting 'mullered' back home.

'Mullered', 'mullahed' – I wouldn't know how you spell it, we're in a dictionary-free zone here. But I know a 'muller' is 'a flat heavy instrument of stone or iron used to grind material against a slab of stone' – and whether that's where it comes from or not, you can tell easy enough anyway, from the sound of it, what getting mullered means. McMahon's soul, certainly, was being ground in a hard place.

Gazza said he wasn't surprised, it was fair enough – and Macca said the same. He said he didn't mind gettng trashed, when they'd played a lousy game – what he hated was getting trashed for two weeks solid beforehand, when the Cup hadn't even started.

'It makes you wonder, are these English people? Do they really want you to win the World Cup? Or would they rather you lost it, so they can sell loads of papers?'

Back in April he told me he read the papers, but not the *Sun*. The *Sun*, after Hillsborough, ran a front page saying THE TRUTH – which was basically lying tittle-tattle leaked through South Yorkshire police trying to cover their backs, that drunken Liverpool fans had been riotous and thieving, and had picked the pockets of the corpses . . . the *Sun*'s circulation fell by 200,000 on Merseyside after that.

Now they'd come to Macca, and offered ten grand for his World Cup story. Macca said to Jon Smith, no way. He said, 'My Dad'd kill me. Everyone in Liverpool would kill me. *I'd* kill me.'

As we went, Gazza couldn't walk past a car that had its driver's window down, without reaching in for a quick parp on the hooter.

But when it came to talking of the game, he was both kind and deadly serious, reaching instead for consolation for McMahon. It had been, he said, 'A cunt of a time to get sent on.'

Together they reached for some cause, some relieving explanation for why the game had gone so badly.

Meanwhile, Robson had gone to Palermo, to watch the Dutch playing Egypt. He had a mate with a private plane who was going to fly him around, but he hadn't turned up yet so he'd gone with the press. (Of which Kirton said, 'He's completely daft, isn't he?')

And in his absence, it was a post-match rest day. Other players were on the golf course; I settled down with Macca and Gazza to get some beers in.

People say that footballers are greedy – but I never found it. You couldn't buy a round with these guys if you tried.

I'd said to McMahon, at Anfield in April, that people saw him as a battler, a fighter.

But he told me, 'I don't like particularly to be thought of in that way, I feel as though I do a lot more – I wouldn't get picked for England just for being a battler. You can get someone off the street to do that.'

And the way he played for Liverpool, and for England – he wasn't the man you'd expect to make the big mistake.

But he also did say about Group F, 'Football's so unpredictable . . . they're all going to be very, very difficult games.'

And I'd asked, back in April, if he had any superstitions. He said, 'I always try to go out after the No. 9 shirt. I don't know why, but I've been doing it for years and years. That's the only one.'

But now, in June, he was a man in pain – and any superstition, any little thing that would help put that nightmare mistake behind him . . . it had been, he said, his thirteenth cap.

And before the game, Gazza then said quickly, warming to the soothing balm of that theme, they'd been kept waiting exactly thirteen minutes before going out . . . as soon as you started looking, there were thirteens everywhere.

Way before that though, Gazza said of Ireland, 'They're going away happy – but there's no way I could go happy from a game that's ones all. No way. No matter what match it is.'

I said, we nearly had them . . .

'Unluckily for us,' said Macca, 'we lost the game. We threw the game away. Or if you want, make it . . . if you want to be harsh, I threw the game away. Which is the way it happened. So the Republic go away thinking that they've got a valuable point. 'Cos they were getting beat 1–0.'

'But you shouldn't look happy,' said Gazza, 'if you're a professional footballer, you shouldn't look happy. If McEnroe got beat by Boris Becker three sets to two, he's not going to think, well, I got two sets . . . 'cos I mean, if it was the other way round, and we scored with fifteen minutes left, we're not going to go round saying, *yeeeaah*, we drew against the Irish. We're going to go away thinking, could have had that.'

Macca stopped him and said, 'Yeah, we could have won it. But,' he reassured himself, 'we're happy with the point.'

So I told him how Robson had said, at the conference afterwards, that the team had to take responsibility for it being 1–1 – that it wasn't an individual thing.

'Well, I don't think . . . not really. At the end of the day, it's an individual mistake, isn't it? But it's a team game, and overall . . . I could easily say, if I wanted to, why didn't they make it 2–0, while the team were playing? Why didn't they make it 3–0? But, you know . . .'

They both agreed that it should have been 2–0 – that the penalty was indisputable.

Then I said, Robson at press conferences defended his players, he supported his players . . .

Macca asked, 'In what way does he support the players?'

He backs you up. When the flak's flying he backs you up, doesn't he?

'I don't know. I don't know. Does he? There's times and

places – I think there's times when he does stick up for the players, and that's brilliant. But there's other times . . .'

Did he say anything to you afterwards?

'Not much, no – there's not a lot he can say. I've held my hands up, I've said . . . he come over and he said, "Anything to say to me, son?" And I says, well, yeah, I apologise, I'm sorry, it was my fault, I've made a mistake – and he went, "OK". In other words, I shouldn't need to be . . . I know I did, but I shouldn't have to be apologising to anybody. That was a genuine mistake, I didn't *want* to give a goal away – I didn't go out and say, there, go and have a goal, Kevin Sheedy, let's make it one each. Everybody knows that. It was just a genuine mistake. And the lads are brilliant – that's just the way it was.'

So everybody says, so be it?

'No one's above everyone else. We all play in the same league. Some players individually are better than others but that doesn't matter, we're in a team together, nobody's on a pedestal – or if they think they are, they'd soon get knocked off it. We're all the same.'

And Gazza said too, 'No one in this squad is above anyone else' – Paul Gascoigne said that? He really was learning.

Because when I quoted Tom Finney saying how in his day he was paid to score goals, not to climb the perimeter fence afterwards, then said that he, Gazza, had been criticised for overdoing it after his last-gasp goal against the Czechs – he said, 'I was going to my dad, wasn't I? I knew where he was sitting. And what do they expect from us? Scoring's what you work for all your life, it's what the people come to see.' So of course you go daft.

Then he said another sweet thing; he said, 'You look at professional footballers – every professional footballer *loves the game*.'

And the reason it's sweet, is that it's simply not a true statement. There are professional footballers who *hate* the game – Peter Beardsley had told me there were people even at Liverpool who hated it, hated the pressure, couldn't wait for quarter to five every Saturday afternoon . . . so it wasn't a true statement.

But Gazza would never understand how it couldn't be true – because it was true about him.

And he talked a lot, that afternoon, about 'being a professional footballer' – as if, just turned twenty-three, and playing first-choice for England in the World Cup in Italy, there was a piece of him that still didn't quite believe he really was one.

So he was learning, and he was loving it – because he loves the game. And with Gazza enjoying himself, and a beer or two inside you – it soon enough cheers you up.

Macca said, it had been a bad game, and he'd made a mistake – but he'd still got a cap, hadn't he?

Platt, Bull, Seaman, Woods, Mike Kelly and others came in off the golf course. As people sat down and ordered their beers, Jack Wiseman took time out from watching Belgium score two against South Korea to organise a golf tournament. On the day after the Holland game, he wanted each player and member of staff to play a round against one of their Sardinian hosts – the staff going out first, and then the players later, when they'd got up and felt recovered.

I'm not sure how eagerly people went for that one . . . but Gazza went eagerly for a £50 bet with David Seaman. There was one of the tees not too far off from the clubroom; and then the green for a different hole was, in turn, not much further from that tee. Between the pin and the tee, there was just a steep slope down, and then a smallish strip of water – and the bet was on who, in three shots, could drop their ball nearest the pin.

So we went out on the balcony to watch. Gazza's first shot was a disaster; he barely cuffed the ball, it skidded off along the tee, and rolled away down the slope towards the water. To loud guffaws along the balcony, he leapt into a buggy standing nearby, and careered off down the precipitous slope to retrieve his ball, like something out of the daffier section of a Bond movie. Seaman, meanwhile, dropped his first attempt just a few yards from the pin. Other players grinned; Gazza, they said, could kiss his fifty goodbye.

He veered back up off the slope, pranced out of the cart, and planted his ball on the tee. You watch, said Platt and Stevens, you watch the Gazza twitch. He took up a stiff stance, raising and lowering his club over the ball, knees jerking, body bobbing over the tee each time – and people counted, laughing, nine, ten, eleven . . . then he put the head of the club softly and perfectly through the ball, and dropped it mere inches from the pin. Seaman conceded his fifty.

Butcher, inside, was quiet. He'd shaved, he said, because he was 'under orders'. He had an ugly purple contusion the size of a big coin round his left eye – he'd had, he said, a few 'clashes' with Cascarino.

Macca said, 'Custer's last stand, that was.'

Gazza came back in looking thoroughly cheerful, winding up Platt about his boss at Villa. 'Dougin' Ellis,' he cackled, 'Dooouuhhgin' Ellis.'

Platt said he couldn't wait to introduce them, next time Villa played Spurs.

Gazza mimed out how he'd greet Ellis, with a wildly exaggerated deference and humility.

Others were winding Bull up. There was a poll back home, they told him, people wanted him to play. Nah, said Bully quietly, he wasn't having that – he took it carefully, like he wasn't quite part of the gang yet, and like he knew the pounce was coming any minute.

Sure enough – 'Take no notice, Bully, they're only polling Wolves and Brummies, aren't they?'

Bull said – when people said Genoa were after him – nah, he wouldn't come and play in Italy. Been on pasta three weeks already, it was enough, he was getting a pot as it was.

Macca showed off how tanned his chest was again.

So Gazza felt obliged to look inside his shorts, to see how tanned his cock was.

It was all cheerful, mannish, impenetrable – a football squad, Kirton had said, was 'a self-regulating unit'. They have their own rhythm, their own language, their own names – a shared, sealed, exclusive group cohesion.

And it was, in fact, impressive. They were riding over the disappointment of the draw with Ireland, turning themselves round, getting ready for the next one . . . so I set off back to Cagliari, my hopes a little lifted.

I hitched back; it took four rides. The last was swerving mayhem in a battered farm van with an amiably irascible village man who, to my surprise, started laying into the press with more venom than the whole England squad combined. The papers, he said, were *cattivi* . . . the English and the Irish were fine by him, no problem at all.

But McMahon had told me a sad story of how far, now, the hooligan psychosis had gone. Four scousers he knew, nice people, had turned up at Is Molas to say hi to him. He'd got the people at the hotel to help, and they'd found them a cheap place to stay down by the beach. And there were only these four from England, staying in this place – yet every morning, the police turned up to check they hadn't rioted yet.

In town, all the bars were shut – *Aida* was on in the amphitheatre. So I went to the Italia and called Roy Collins's room; he would surely, I thought, be watching Egypt–Holland, that game being somewhat relevant to our prospects.

But it looked to me, when I got to his room, like the man had crashed out – which was a little unfair on the Egyptians, who came very close indeed to doing another Cameroon. Once more, you might say, with African feeling . . . they could have had three before the Dutch scored in the fifty-eighth – and they did get one anyway, with a penalty near the end. It was another really iffy decision – the guy was fouled outside the area, and had to work pretty hard before falling down in it – but it was justice all the same: Egypt 1, Holland 1.

In Cairo, two died in the manic celebrations that followed this excellent performance. And the police officer in charge of that city's deranged traffic said he was pleased it had only been a draw – if they'd won, he said, there'd have been a revolution.

So now each team in Group F had one point, one goal – and while things unfolded all over Italy, no one here on the islands had gone anywhere.

There was, however, this one small difference between the two islands in question: that on Sardinia, we looked like Sodbury Mechanicals could wallop us on an off day – whereas in Sicily the Egyptians looked great, and the Dutch . . . well, they had their problems. But they were still the Dutch, weren't they?

Collins, meanwhile, blearily raged and raved about 'fucking cunting Eyeties'. The COL and Olivetti inefficiencies, and the general reluctance of the Italians to print a ticket for any match that wasn't kicking off in the next five minutes, were getting badly up his nose – and so was the booze ban.

It was a comical thing, all these English journos who'd clamoured for booze bans to keep the dreadful hoolies in line, now finding to their horror that there were indeed booze bans – and that they applied to them too. Collins was urgent about the prime necessity of locating a place that'd give him wine for lunch on the next match day. He said, 'I can go a day without a drink, two days even – but I won't be *told* I can't drink.'

So I took him to the Trattoria La Taverna, where the unendingly friendly couple who ran the place put his dark fears to rest – lunch could be had on the day of the Holland game, and wine could be had with it.

In the process, Collins's wish to learn the languages of the countries he worked in ('beer one' in Seoul now seeming more a dypsomaniac necessity, than a cultural acquisition) turned out to extend only so far as the creation of a monstrous pidgin. His English accent rode through a chaos of random words and syntax – brutishly proud, and lazily unaltered.

Pedro! Spiros! Luigi!

England 1, Ireland 1.

Ghastly press, oafish fans, and 4–4–2 . . . all played out.

It would, I thought, take one of two things for England to get past the dangerous Dutch, and then the splendid Egyptians.

It was either going to take a revolution in the way we played football.

Or it was going to take the likes of John Barnes to wake up and come good.

Revolution

England–Holland

'What do we need this sweeper for?'
– Bobby Robson, November '89

I flew back into Cagliari with yet another Wolves fan (they were everywhere). He was a bright bloke – and he had a word for Dave Hill on his John Barnes book.

'What's wrong with that book comes out at the end, where he goes back and describes Barnes going past one man, two men again, and he says, Jamaica-style. If he'd have said, Barnes-style, OK. What's Jamaica got to do with it?'

He was, he said, a football fan first, a Wolves fan second. He was in Italy for three weeks and seven games, and reckoning to spend £2,500 in that time. He couldn't afford it, though he had a good job – he ran a video label – but he said by '94 he'd be thirty-four years old, he might have kids, who knows? He'd never done a World Cup, and this was his chance.

It was three out of his year's four weeks' holiday – he'd already spent the rest following Wolves, when they went near to promotion. He didn't go to every game – 'I'm not a trainspotter' – but he had a good time; and now this was even better. No trouble, great country, big pleasure – and just one gripe: tickets.

On Saturday 2 June his travel agent took the cash in person to the FA – and they were shut. She posted it through the letterbox, and called Monday – and they'd sent the tickets in the post. No, she cried, don't, I'll send a bike – too late. He got them three days before he left on 11 June – 'it was bloody worrying'. He'd paid in April.

The people he was with didn't get theirs in time; their wives sent them on. He said, to be fair, he knew the Italians had released the tickets very late; and the FA had been very helpful. But you pay a lot of money for these holidays, and this was stuff you seriously didn't need, calling agents all the time, finding the FA office, getting transport into Cagliari – when the place you were staying in was ninety kilometres away.

And he knew, too, of people in his business being offered sponsor's tickets for the semis and the final, who just weren't interested – the 'blue suit and champagne brigade' – when he was out *begging* for these things.

The likes of Mars and Gillette took 2,000 people to Italia '90, minimum; I knew an agent in Manchester who proudly boasted how he had 15,000 bookings from sponsors . . . and he got his tickets all right.

So who owns this game?

Not the millions of poor sods who pay for it, that's for sure.

And of course your truly hard money man could turn round and say, with TV and related marketing, we could play matches in empty stadiums and still come out smiling . . . but it wouldn't be football, would it?

Two pressmen gave me a lift in their cab from the airport to the training ground at Pula. A busload of eccentric Dutch industrial machine reps turned up; they were all uniformed in orange suits and straw boaters, with orange-white-blue weskits and bow ties. Robson had met them in Palermo, and invited them along to get some FA knick-knacks.

But these cheerful souls couldn't lighten the atmosphere in the England camp; the national grid firing up every floodlight on earth couldn't have cast light into the black heart of matters now.

The Hostess Isabella story had broken.

The *Mirror* intimated that three players – unnamed, of course, or the libel wallop would have been mighty indeed – had late night disco and after hours nookie with a local COL stewardess, who'd subsequently been moved from Is Molas to the furthest hotel down the road.

Oddly, the genesis of this bilious malice was a football man from one of the qualities – acknowledged by a colleague to be 'a fantasist' – who'd put himself both professionally and personally in danger, by trying to sell his invention to the *Sun*. Professionally, for the obvious reasons – and personally, because the Hostess Isabella's brother was now muttering darkly about taking the man off into the mountains for a terminal taste of his hunting rifle.

And just to prove the story was crap – the *Sun* turned it down. When the *Mirror* bit instead, the *Sun* were then able to spin round on them with this glorious headline:

> MORE LIES FROM FAT MAX
> Maxwell, 22 stone . . .

They may be bastards – but they can be funny bastards on their day.

Not, however, if you're the Hostess Isabella. The rotters were hounding the poor girl all over Cagliari – when her only crime had been to speak inadequate English for the job at Is Molas and, anyhow, to be transferred is a matter of routine on the COL work roster. But that's the tabloids for you. One minute your languages aren't up to scratch – the next, you've been out fucking footballers. And like policemen, once they've decided you've done a thing, they'll hound you until they've extracted the confession . . . one Brian McNally, senior sports writer on a Newcastle paper, tried to protect the girl – and, amazingly, was threatened with being reported to the NUJ for 'impeding journalists in the course of their duty'.

The great majority of the football men – including the helplessly shamefaced souls from the quarter of the gutter that printed this muck – tried as best as they could to dissociate themselves from it. Patrick Barclay said he wasn't surprised the players had gone on quote strike – he said there'd been football men who felt like going out in sympathy. (Though another told me later, 'Well, Paddy – he's always good for a reaction.')

But dissociate as you may, it wouldn't do you much good – because from the players' point of view, this was just the biggest piece of shit yet in a long-building tunnel of press sewage. Journalists – they were all the fucking same.

With a weary contempt Robson told the BBC, 'It's pretty

dismal reporting – 'cos there's no truth in it. What are they trying to do? Torpedo the players, torpedo the team? It's a diabolical game to play.'

John Barnes walked back across the training pitch to the bus, turning away questions. 'No,' he said, polite but definite, 'I'm disillusioned, you know? Disillusioned with life, you know what I mean?'

I asked David Bloomfield what had happened; he told me the story, and pointed out the *Mirror*'s John Jackson, known among the press pack as Chief Rotter. Bloomfield said, with bitter irony, 'It was that cunt in the Fair Play T-shirt. Rich, that.'

Tickets for the Mirror Group's reporters had, it seemed, mysteriously failed to appear . . .

Terry Butcher was feeling doubly aggrieved. Not only were the front pages slopping over with toxin; but on the back pages it was BUTCHER AXED, too.

I asked, 'Are you?'

He grinned grimly and said, 'No.'

Something was wrong with the Dutch.

While the English camp was united against their tabloid tormentors, the Dutch camp was, by all accounts, deeply disunited – and had been for months. Ruud Gullit, during his year off injured, said when he saw his national side play, it 'made his toes curl'. Dark rumours of player power – or certainly, of player disgruntlement – seemed confirmed when the manager who'd seen them through qualification, Thijs Libregts, was replaced by Leo Beenhakker of Ajax only weeks before the tournament. Trouble was, the players didn't want him either – they'd wanted Johan Cruyff.

Still, managerial mayhem needn't necessarily screw you over. The Yugoslav Velibor 'Bora' Milutinovic was Costa Rica's fourth manager in two years – and look what happened to them.

But Holland had other problems. Gullit had only played in AC Milan's last two League games of the Italian season; he wasn't match-fit, while his clubmates Rijkaard and Van Basten were match-drained. They'd had an exhausting time of it, winning the European Cup late in May – but seeing their domestic League and Cup hopes blow up in their faces. So was the spine of the Dutch team knackered?

They'd only played four friendlies together, since they were beaten by Brazil in December – they'd drawn with Italy, and lost to the Russians and the Austrians. But then, on 3 June, they went to Zagreb, and tonked Yugoslavia 2–0. The world smiled knowingly; Gullit was back – and internal strife, that was the Dutch way, wasn't it? Didn't they always argue like hell with each other until kick-off, then scorch their opponents, when it came to the real thing, like they were working it out of their system? Look out, we all said – here come the European champions again . . .

On 12 June they worked nothing out of their system: Holland 1. Egypt 1.

Gullit said, 'We were always running, but never with the ball. And I played very bad. The mind wants more than the body, the body isn't ready to do such work . . . sometimes I want to do more than I can.'

And Beenhakker said, 'We all know we have good players in Holland; but we don't have a good team at the moment.'

Robson wasn't buying any of this. For a start, who said Egypt would be easy? He told the Dutch press, 'I've seen Egypt play five, six times – and I've never seen them lose. They have five or six very good players, very good.'

And few knew better than he did how well the Dutch could play. In Germany we'd held the line with them for maybe seventy minutes – then they spanked us 3–1. Van Basten, thought Robson, was 'electric'.

Harry Harris grinned and said we should play Steve Bull. 'Koeman won't fancy some hairy-arsed skinhead charging up his backside.'

The press said Butcher would be dropped, because they knew how badly Robson feared the incisive pace of the Dutch. So how could he make the creaky 4–4–2 less creaky? By playing Wright at the back instead, he was faster – and by playing Paul Parker for the too-orthodox Gary Stevens, because he was fast too, and as good a limpet-like man-marker as we had.

Not that it really mattered. Playing the way we played, if the Dutch woke up they'd tear through us anyway, whoever the back four were.

*

I went on from training to Is Molas, and had lunch with Jane Nottage and Giacomo Malvermi. They had faxes of the latest tabloid bile; in response to Robson's disgusted denials of the Isabella thing, the *Mirror* had now run a self-serving editorial titled, 'Over The Top', in which Maxwell's true purpose was revealed: Get Robson. The piece was a merciless onslaught on his managerial competence – and you thought, we've only played one game . . .

Giacomo Malvermi was a hoot. And you can laugh – Naked Hostess Turned Into Olive Shock, COL Girl Found On Moon Horror – but the atmosphere was wearily angry and disbelieving. Among the players, anyhow.

Malvermi attempted to teach Bloomfield how to say in Italian, 'I am drowning in the perfection of your loveliness,' in case he should chance upon a Hostess Isabella of his own.

Graham Kelly and some BBC types pottered about with tennis racquets. Giacomo said they were crazy, to play at three in the afternoon in Sardinia. Mad dogs and English newspapers . . . and like I say, you can laugh.

But could the families of twenty-two footballers back home laugh? Could Isabella's family laugh? She was reported variously to be twenty, twenty-five, twenty-seven . . . if you can't get her age right, what chance the poor girl's private life?

Outside, Jon Smith cooked in peace by the pool. 'This,' he said, in his postage stamp trunks, 'is the best part of my job.' He'd been busy round Italy, fixing for Argentina to visit Wembley in May '91, then the Germans the following September; and he'd been checking in with the FIFA moguls in Rome. In their offices he heard a torrent of calls coming in, complaining about the refereeing of Erik Fredriksson – the man was being sent home.

And there was, he said, some uncertainty about what might happen with the Russians by the time we came to 1994. Would Lithuania have an independent football team? He joked grimly, 'Instead of playing the USSR, it'll just be the SSR. Or the SR.' Still, never mind – business was booming out on Planet Football.

So was politics. Moynihan was expected in tomorrow for the match, and then for a security meeting Sunday morning to assess what the fans had got up to. Nottage was booking herself into Is Molas for the night, so she could be on hand to help out with the little man's media needs.

'A new Pamella Bordes,' said Malvermi, 'that's what the media needs. Let's shop her – let's get on the blower to John Jackson right now. COL Official Bonks Minuscule For Sport Shock.'

'I give up,' said Nottage, 'I'll ring him myself. The entire England team are in bed with Miss Nigeria . . . I'm having Sunday off. I've fucking had it with those people.'

Bloomfield pulled himself out of the pool, and grinned in the sun. 'What a crap job, eh?'

From the team meeting in the games room came the sound of Robson going through videos of England and Holland, and urgent, uptight little snatches of talk: 'Where were we? There's nobody there . . .'

Bloomfield said Shilton and Lineker, the two men from Leicester who roomed together, were running a book on each match together too; taking bets on who'd win and who'd lose, on scores at half-time and full-time . . . he said Gazza was a couple of hundred quid up. If the boy fell down the toilet, he'd come out smelling of Chanel.

And while we lay by the pool, Bobby Robson – in fear of Van Basten and some other flying Dutchman coming steaming through the middle – planned, almost unwittingly, the revolution that helped make England one of the three best football teams in the world.

After the team meeting, I sat with Terry Butcher in the room he shared with Chris Woods, waiting for Austria–Czechoslovakia to come on at five. They were tiny and spartan rooms, too – just space for the two beds, and leg-room to walk around them.

Butcher reckoned they'd done OK against the Irish; and from his own point of view, given the amount of time he spent heading away high ball after high ball, that was probably fair enough. But he also said, 'Typical British game – there wasn't any football to be played.'

Gullit had excused us for that. He said, 'That's not a normal game – with the sentimental things there, that's just fighting, they don't want to lose. England–Ireland – that's something else.'

Butcher said, 'Against the Dutch, it'll be a bit more cultured.

And I look forward to that more – from a football point of view, it'll be a lot better.'

I asked what Robson had told them to do.

'Win.'

But could we?

'Wouldn't be here if we didn't think we could beat them. The Dutch won't go into the game as confident, perhaps, as they were – the Egyptians played very well – and we owe them a good game after Germany anyway. People look at it and say Holland are favourites, and it makes you very angry, you know – people go on about the Dutch players here in Italy, or Spain, and they've got Kieft going to Bordeaux now . . . but haven't we got good players? We just keep knocking ourselves down all the time.'

Butcher didn't play in Germany '88, he had a broken leg – so he went with his family to America. He said, 'I couldn't have watched it. Not sat at home.'

Then he looked up and said, 'Oi, Woodsy – there's a spider.' He then explained, 'He's a spider-killer,' as Woods flattened the hapless arachnid. Butcher said, 'We have a bug inspection every night.'

'Any little crawling thing,' said Woods, 'I hate 'em.'

The game began; Butcher said the Czechs had been difficult at Wembley. 'They thought because they were big they had the right to walk all over you. They didn't like it when you got stuck into them though – they didn't fancy it then.' But they were behind the Czechs anyhow as a dud game unfolded.

The only goal came on the half-hour. Lindenberger, wearing his acid house zebra crossing again, brought Chovanec down with a fair imitation of a rugby tackle; Woods said, 'I'm not having that.' While Chovanec was carried off to lie by the hoardings, Bilek won the game from the spot. As he took the penalty, he slipped and fell; Woods and Butcher roared at that.

Chovanec was taken away on a stretcher with his thigh strapped, and the cameras followed him down the tunnel. 'kin' hell,' Butcher grumbled, 'they'll be in the bloody hospital with you next.'

Woods made predictions at every free-kick – left foot, right foot, over the wall, or bending round it. 'These new balls here,' he said, 'they really fly.'

Butcher watched in a less technical frame of mind. 'He was going to stay down there. Cheat. Angers me, when people stay down.'

He'd got a phrase book, and it was *buongiorno* all over the place. Like a big friendly bear, he was getting on famously with the staff; every time they did something, it was, '*Grazie*. Top man.'

At half-time we went to get some tea at the bar. Don Howe was sat with Dennis Howell, Labour's Minister of Sport in the distant days before Thatcher – and Howe asked Terry to get some tea for them too. As we went back down the corridor he muttered, 'What's the matter with him then? Did he break both his legs?'

The game dragged on; we lost interest, and talked about the other matches. Woods said, 'Did you see, Maradona admitted the handball this time?'

'D'you think he was under pressure to, or what?'

I told them what a dud Italy–USA had been. Woods said, 'That's like us playing Motherwell though – they all sit back, make it hard for you.'

Meanwhile, the Czechs looked good; the only reason they didn't get more was the Austrians kept upending them (something for the Americans to look forward to there). They had a fair following of fans, too, in this new European home. One had a serious gut on him; Butcher said, 'I bet he stinks. They all fuckin' stink, East European countries. It's, oooph – *omnipresent* . . .'

The Czechs joined Italy and Cameroon in the second phase; and Austria joined the USA and Russia at the unhappy door marked Exit.

Woods ran through the permutations of who might end up where – and there was a chance, if England went through in third place, that we'd end up in Milan. He said, 'I fancy the San Siro. Who'd we get there?'

The Germans.

'Maybe I don't fancy it.'

Butcher said, 'I hate the fuckin' Germans.'

Then Trevor Steven and Gary Stevens came in to get a card game under way; that aura of single-minded exclusivity that footballers can wrap about themselves settled in once again. Twenty-four hours to go until the bus turned up with its escort at the Sant'Elia for the second time . . . so I left, and hitched a ride back into Cagliari.

And at nine that evening the Germans, having put four past Yugoslavia, went out and put five more past the United Arab Emirates. They too were now qualified for the second phase – and they looked by far the best team in it too. Adroit tap-ins, fierce headers, rockets from long range – they didn't mind how they did it, and they kept on doing it. They could have had ten – Klinsmann and Völler were rapier-sharp up front, and Matthäus untiringly powerful through the middle. If they carried on like this, who could stop them?

I watched this massacre with Rogan Taylor and John Williams in the Italia. Then afterwards, we went to check out the eve-of-match festivities – and there weren't any. There were more photographers than fans, and more police than both together. The police had told regular bars they couldn't screen the matches on their TVs any more . . . Cagliari was turning into a ghost town.

And so to another alcohol-free match day . . .

England–Holland was, in theory, the Group F biggie – the head-to-head to decide who'd come out on top. But in theory, both sides should have had two points by then anyhow.

It was the big one off the pitch, too. The press had been awash for months with hysterical tales of English and Dutch ringleaders getting together to draw up their rules of engagement, or of how the Dutch bad boys planned on bringing bombs to the stadium. Hooligan psychosis – the police were ubiquitous, and oppressive.

There'd been 5,000 English, maximum, for the Ireland game; now, for Holland, they expected two or three thousand more. They reckoned on seven or eight thousand Dutch, too – 3,000 coming on twenty-two charters from Palermo; plenty more by boat.

I went to a conference for the rotters in a drab building by the COL offices on the industrial estate; it was held in a barren and echoey little hall, with the dismal feel about it of an unused bus station. The embassy, and the rotters with it, were keeping a daily tally of arrests and deportations – there had been relatively few, and in the villains league the Germans were ahead at that time. Kay Coombes from the embassy, and Moynihan's press man, both tried drumming home to the rotters the difference between detention and arrest – if you were taken in for an hour or two, questioned and released, that didn't constitute an arrest under Italian or any other kind of law . . . but in *Sun* law, it did.

The Home Secretary had given a list to the Italians of about a hundred whose entry they should bar. Several had been picked up on their way through Rome and sent home. Most prominent among these, a day or two back, was the well-known nerd Paul Scarrot, who'd been scraped off the railway lines at Roma Termini with an empty five-litre flagon of wine, loudly blathering about the mayhem he planned to wreak. The state he was in, he couldn't have planned on getting his cock out of his trousers to piss with it – and it was powerfully rumoured that he'd circumvented his banning orders with the assistance of a tabloid. Serious hoolies, after all, do not give interviews, or seek their photographs on the front pages.

A man who'd given his name as 'Mr Kent Sevenoaks', Coombes wryly announced, had been picked up at Olbia with twenty grams of dope, and sent home too.

An English fan who'd been set on by locals was in hospital, with bruising and head injuries.

There had been, last night, just a few minor incidents, and no arrests.

A delegation of photographers had been to see the police, seeking an agreement whereby they'd stop getting whacked as they went about their business. Little hope was expressed that the agreement would hold.

The prefect had confirmed – in response to a letter from Moynihan – that there would, this time, be buses laid on after the game.

The minister's man then said a report that the minister had been refused a drink at Milan airport on his way here was untrue. Firstly, he hadn't asked for one. Secondly, he'd gone via Genoa.

'And he doesn't drink anyway?' a rotter idly inquired.

'Absolutely not. Not during the World Cup, anyway. Just like you boys. Just like all of you.'

I went and had the lunch we'd reserved at La Taverna with

Roy Collins, and two other fine specimens of the genus Chief Sports Writer. As the wine went down Collins said, 'I should write a piece saying the drinks ban should be more stringently enforced. In my case anyway. "Please Stop Me Drinking" . . . but no, I can't do this without drinking. I'd go mad.'

Another of them – unbelievable fat bastard – then came up with a virulent condemnation of Robson's behaviour in his private life. What he found especially disgusting, he said, was that Robson had had the extra-curricular in his own marital bed.

In the next breath he then informed us that he'd had a bit of the extra-curricular himself once, in his family car – as if that was OK. And with crocodile tears he said the guilt (ha ha) had made him sell it. He sniggered grossly and said, 'It was a pokey little runner, too.'

These brave and red-eyed boys, getting ready over the clandestine grape to write clear-headed reports for the customers back home, were sitting already on some serious hangovers. They'd played, as they put it, seventeen holes last night, and got nowhere – until they found the Bar Marius open, and then a club. They'd got pissed enough to argue about being thrown out early – at 5.30 in the morning . . . and the *fans* behave badly?

One of them said he needed a fruit salad, he didn't want to get scurvy.

'That's rich,' said Collins, 'he had fourteen hundred whiskies last night, his liver's exploding – and he's worried about scurvy.'

World Cup Party? *Festa*?

Cagliari was eerie. By three in the afternoon, the town seemed totally shut down. A chopper hung noisy and low in an ugly, lowering sky over Via Roma. There was a cold wind getting up; the two open cafés in the arcade were sparsely populated. Little draggles of fans drifted around looking lost and small. I met a group of Brummies who were staying at the other end of the island, who'd hired a minibus for the eight-hour ride each way to and from the game – it was better that way, they said. Who wants to spend a fortnight under martial law?

I sat drinking coffee and mineral water with some of the boys I'd met before. And then, I thought, a-hah! – here at last come two likely looking lads, two terrifying English storm-troopers, two members of the army of villainous and violent men Jeff Powell had warned the Italians to expect . . . they sat down at the table next to us.

They were both big, strong, tanned, well-muscled and wholly mean-looking guys. One, the bulkier, had a cropped boulder for a skull; the other, taller and broader, sported glinting US bike-cop shades. They ordered Cokes, and topped them up with Jack Daniels from a bottle in their bag. They wore sawn-off T-shirts, with torn strips of blue scarf tied round taut and bulging biceps. The shirts said on the front 'Lean Mean Blue Machine'; on the back, 'Bad Blue Boys'.

A Barnsley lad on my table leant bravely their way and asked, 'You Chelsea?'

'No,' said the guy in shades, with a voice like a rock slide and a clotted Slavic accent, 'we're Dynamo Zagreb.'

I must have laughed the only laugh in Cagliari all day . . .

And still the heavy silence hung over town, broken only by helicopters or the shriek of police sirens – it was like waiting for war. I counted my cigarettes before leaving for the ground (the *tabachi* were shut as well as the bars, prompting one fan to ask, what they think we're gonna do, run apeshit on nicotine?) Nervously, recalling McMahon and Gascoigne's superstition attack, I found I had *thirteen* . . .

On the way to the ground, there were noticeably more girls among the Dutch support than among the English. Everything about them was orange, from T-shirts to shoes; even orange lip-stick.

Four big ferries were stacked up in dock, waiting to get them back out to Palermo.

People were buying tickets off touts all the way along the route; cars would pull up, and tickets be offered out the windows.

I passed a boy with 'Made In Burnley' tattooed on his left shoulderblade, and the England shield with 'Italy '90' beneath it on the right. As we went past two vanloads of *carabinieri*, his mate waved and smiled at them; he said quietly under his breath, 'We see you later, kick your fucking heads in.'

Would it go off then, today? The appalling idiot Chris

Wright – the man in the top hat – was going round making himself feel big again, telling the boys to march on the stadium from the station at six.

At the ground, there were 1,500 police, military, and *carabinieri* – thousands more round town.

And you thought to yourself, I could be partying with Brazil in Turin, or with Cameroon in Bari – it had got to where people joked with relief, now, when they flew out to report on mainland matches: I'm off to the World Cup. Whereas England, we were football in quarantine – and lousy football too . . .

It looked like another thunderstorm was coming. It was humid and windy; through the forest of stubby trees and shiny new yellow lamposts in the Sant'Elia parking lot, the mountains across the bay were just dim shapes beneath a heavy blue darkness. A couple of minutes into Brazil–Costa Rica at five, the monitors in the press centre went down.

And news began coming in that the English march to the stadium had turned into a riot.

There were no Dutch involved. The Italians had met the march with a wall of police, and diverted it on to wasteground where there was rubble to hand. Rocks began to fly, and *whoomph* – tear gas and baton charge. People who'd come from there said it was major over-reaction. An estimated three hundred – seemingly an arbitrary group – were now penned in a gas station. There were worries for these people – journalists had been *sent away* . . .

Meanwhile the TV picture was recovered, and Brazil went one ahead after thirty-three minutes. Costa Rica were unlucky – Muller's strike took an awkward deflection – but this, surely, would now turn into another German-style monster-eats-minnow, spitting out goals like fishbones.

The corner count in the first half was Brazil 9, Costa Rica 0. In the second half too, the Brazilians set up camp in the Costa Rican penalty area – yet the supposed no-hopers defended with a maximum of bravery and effort; they kept it to 1–0 right through to the end.

The Brazilians, it seemed, had the Italian problem, that pretty patterns and fine passes do not alone make goals – that you need a man on the end of your finery who knows where the net is. And the frustration began to show; it was a clean and dive-free game until, near the end, the Costa Ricans had the guileless audacity to start slipping their opposite numbers – so the Brazilians Jorginho and Mozer both got booked, one for hacking at passing knees, the other for an elbow to a passing face.

So we were in for an instructive contrast here tonight . . . and while we waited, rumoursome news came in from the riot zone – of cars overturned and burned, of hundreds arrested.

None of it was true.

The fool Chris Wright, we later learnt, was going round declaiming that a fan and a policeman had been shot. The land of hysterical fantasy.

The weather cleared; it was hot and dry again. The sun went down over the bay, a brilliant orange disc between the mountains to the left, and medieval Cagliari on its hill to the right; the helicopters clattered back and forth in between.

In the stadium a Union Jack defiantly stated: Swindon Town Will Never Die. And there they all were, Aston Villa, Bristol City, Rochdale, Salford, Chester, Millwall, Lincoln and Leicester, Coventry and Notting Hill . . . We Are England.

But we're European too. Bobby Robson, like Brazil, was playing a sweeper . . . around the press box, people looked at the new back line with a strange mix of satisfaction, trepidation, and disbelief. They looked as if they'd been kidnapped and deposited in a whole new quadrant of Planet Football where the geography was unknown, the ground underfoot unsteady, and the compass readings wild and unreliable.

In the build-up, the headline approach had been the axing of Butcher; people figured Wright would play in his stead. Others, to be fair – not a few others – had scratched heads and thought, maybe he really might do it. But surely not . . . Bobby Robson abandon 4–4–2? It was like the queen in a miniskirt.

On the morning of the game, Patrick Barclay wrote that if it were to happen, 'By Robson's standards it would be almost revolutionary . . . we must wait and see.' So now we'd waited, we looked, and we saw.

First reactions could be summed up as Laurel and Hardy – that's a fine system you've gotten me into. Because while the smarter minority among them had hammered away for some time for us to join Europe in the modern world, and start playing this way – even so, wasn't the second and toughest group game in the first round of the World Cup a pretty drastic, late-in-the-day sort of time to find out if it would work?

The guy next to me said, 'It'll work if Holland don't score.'

But it was England who made the first impression – Butcher, of all people, going forward to release Lineker. I felt too gnawed with tension to write much; I could only note how good, how imaginative, how intelligent the football now seemed. *The ball stayed on the ground* . . . and England looked sharp, winning the first corner after Barnes, this time, set Lineker free once more with a slide-rule pass that ran through the middle like it was computer-guided. Then Gascoigne streaked through two defenders; his cross found Bryan Robson's head, and flew wide. And Barnes was showing his quality; he won a free kick down the left, confounding Barcelona's Ronald Koeman. Gazza whipped the kick across the box; both Wright and Lineker failed to get to it by inches.

They were getting through, when it was supposed to be the Dutch who did that. The back, the middle, the front, everything linked and flowed – and the English fans were loving it.

On our monitors, unbelievably, the Scots went a goal up against the Swedish in Genoa.

And what is football, some days, some nights, but ninety minutes of agony?

Please please score

The Dutch looped in their second corner.

Please please don't let them score

Gascoigne looked hard and bright in the middle; Gullit looked soft and rusty. But the Dutch were beginning to make slim chances, and Gullit missed two; they were linking up, and flowing as we were. Honours even, by the half-hour; they were humming now, winning more corners . . . then Gazza set off from the centre circle, beat three men, and was brought down – not for the first time. He'd have been clear through otherwise.

There's only one Paul Gascoigne
Only one Paw-uhl Gaaaa-uh-scoigne

Half-time, 0–0.

News came in of seven fans taken to hospital. Three were treated for cuts and bruises, then released. One was said to have a broken leg, after being run over by a police vehicle; two others had been severely beaten – and the seventh had escaped on the way there . . . but it had been (of course) not as bad as it looked. Some fifty or a hundred were still detained.

The Dutch went out strong into the second half, and quickly got two corners. For five minutes, for the first time, they looked in control; but only for five minutes. Then Bryan Robson fired a long shot at the other end – and Gazza went on working through the middle, jinking and passing, going back and coming forward, causing no end of trouble of the very best kind.

Pearce and Parker, too, were steaming up the flanks . . . Lineker had two stabs at goal. The first ricocheted away, the second went in – and was disallowed for a handball, the ball striking his elbow as the rebound came back at him. It was as inadvertent as it gets – he should get a new passport off that nice Mr Menem . . . then, five minutes later, working a delicious one-two through the middle with Barnes, he fired the best chance yet high and wide.

The crowd grew buzzy with excitement, as they realised Steve Bull was coming on for Chris Waddle – we were throwing it at them now. Bull's first touch was a header wide; he was annoyed with himself too. Barnes had started it, Lineker made the cross – England were enlivened.

Press opinion was that the Dutch weren't on their game; but a tactical triumph for Bobby Robson all the same.

Then Bryan Robson came off, limping. He had a bad toe, they'd been cutting the impacted nail away where he'd stubbed it in training . . . ugh.

So David Platt went on – and what a first taste of World Cup, to go on against the Dutch in a game that stood so poised and so fluid, and replace the man who all felt was the pumping heart, the inspiration, the leader; but Platt was up to it.

Voices in the box: 'Who's picking this team? Graham Taylor?'

'He's only doing it to give us stories. Platt and Bull are the only two who talk to us.'

It was a new look England – and it looked just great. Rijkaard was shut down, he had little chance to come forward as he wrestled to contain Gascoigne, Barnes, Bull, Lineker, they were everywhere; while Des Walker at the back had nagged Van Basten into an invisible drift. Gullit was a shadow of his '88 self – there was little doubt who the new name was now.

Gazza left two men standing in stone with an immaculate little turn on the by-line; he was there one minute, then span on a sixpence and was gone the next. He clipped in a quick low cross, and Bull and Lineker in turn both missed it by inches.

'Just wish the little shit'd talk to us.'

Like Bobby Robson said – you'd think they were playing for the papers out there . . .

England were solid at the back, and moving forward well-oiled and deft.

All we are saaaa-ying
Give us a goal

Defying all prediction, Scotland did – in Genoa, they went two ahead of Sweden. The Swedes, much fancied outsiders, joined the Russians and the rest on the road back home – while Scotland stayed in it.

And so did we, with a vengeance. You didn't come much more fancied than the Dutch – and they'd blown it. They were tied back now to Koeman taking speculative whacks from thirty-five yards – there was no way through.

Robson had expected Van Basten and Kieft through the middle, and he'd played the sweeper to contain that. Instead, Kieft was on the bench, Van Basten was alone, and Gillhaus was on the wing – but Gillhaus plays for Aberdeen, and Butcher knew all about him. So now the English back line was a rubber sheet, instead of the brittle wall of times past – and any time they came at us, we just bounced right back.

With sixteen minutes left, Kieft did go on – but Butcher, Wright, and Walker had the middle good and locked up by then; England had enjoyed their new shape for too long going forward, for any change to worry them much now.

Let's all have a disco
Let's all have a disco
La la la la
La la la la

In the last minute, Gascoigne set off again. Headed for the by-line on the right, he was obstructed, and fell. Reward: an indirect free-kick. Pearce lined up, and put the ball in the net with venom; but it didn't touch anyone *en route* . . . like Lineker's effort earlier, it too was disallowed.

This was seriously unlucky – because the Dutch keeper, diving, can't have missed it by more than a few inches . . . an odd case where the keeper saved by *not* touching the ball.

So we finished England 0, Holland 0.

But like Beenhakker said, in the second half in particular, England were by some margin the better side. The way we'd played, we'd both erased the Irish horror-hoof – and put down our first marker as contenders for the fourteenth World Cup. It was tentative, compared to the Germans – but a marker nonetheless.

Gullit said, 'It was difficult to control them, and we were lucky to get a draw.'

'What do we need this sweeper for?'

The contrast between England and Brazil playing a five-man back line was this.

It was not, as John Barnes had wistfully said (and as most of Brazil was now angrily saying) the Brazilian way to think defensive. But with over half his squad based in Europe (including ten of the thirteen who played the Costa Ricans) the coach Lazaroni had opted for a European back line – then found, when they wore the gold and green, that it didn't suit them.

As for Robson, his expressed opinion about the system had been brusque, and misleadingly Brazilian: 'Why do we need to play *more* defensive?'

But no system *per se* is offensive or defensive. Whatever the system, you can choose to attack with it, or to sit back and hold tight – and which way you go depends, in the end, on how the players are feeling on the park.

So Brazil laboured. Their touch was sweet as ever – but their front and midfield felt undermanned, and they played all out of kilter. Brazil 1, Costa Rica 0.

The effect on England was entirely the opposite. Brazil weren't used to concentrating on defence; whereas England were freed from being obsessed with it. It was when we played 4–4–2 that we'd been undermanned, both at the back and in midfield – but with Wright as a sweeper making three centre-backs, suddenly the heart of the defence felt hugely less vulnerable.

So instead of Pearce and Gary Stevens feeling constrained to hang back and cover on the flanks (so that Barnes and Waddle in turn felt tied back in front of them) Pearce and the nippy Paul Parker were now liberated to push up, in the knowledge that the heart behind them was more secure. Pearce and Parker became 'wing-backs'; and freed up the likes of Barnes to go roaming, and cause damage wherever he may.

Whether anyone had seen it working quite so positively beforehand is a different matter. Robson did talk at the press conference about the full backs pushing up in offence – but primarily he'd been thinking 'sweeper = more defence'. He did it to stop the Dutch, not to kick-start us – after all, he played 5–4–1, not 3–5–2.

In short, he played a sweeper against Holland because, I have no doubt, he was scared of Van Basten and Kieft ripping through his flat back four.

So you might say, his insecurity won out over his conservatism – the same gritted-teeth insecurity that had driven him to hang in there against the slings and arrows of outrageous tabloids – and it made him play the extra safety card against his own professed beliefs.

And yet the defensive improvement, by making things more secure, also made things more flexible – there was more freedom to attack, more room for invention and variety.

Or, to put it another way, Robson played 5–4–1 – but when you've got the ball, defending 5–4–1 converts with elastic recoil into attacking 3–5–2 in no time at all. And then suddenly you're all over them.

It was an ironic turnabout. Robson stood by 4–4–2 as an attacking system, believing in the class of his two wingers; yet 4–4–2 tied those wingers down because playing that way we had always to scramble back and defend. Then he went out and played a sweeper-based defensive system – and, with the back secured, we ended up doing more of the attacking . . .

The man beside me said before the game, 'It'll work if Holland don't score.'

They didn't; England looked regularly more likely to. They were powerfully unfortunate to get the ball in the net twice, and be denied both times. So the reaction at nine o'clock that it was a pretty hairy time to be trying a sweeper turned, by ten forty-five, to approval.

'England did much more than hold Holland, the European champions, to a draw . . . they redeemed themselves, gave heart to their beleaguered supporters, and made a successful World Cup campaign a real possibility.'

If Brian Glanville could write that, we must have done something right. He called the switch to the new system, 'Astonishing.'

But the approval was conditioned, of course, by the fact that we still hadn't actually scored. Two games, two points – and if either Egypt or Ireland won in Palermo the next day, it'd be them who'd be heading the group . . .

It's worth noting, otherwise, that no one got booked – the referee, a Yugoslavian engineer, had a good game – and then, these two points that came out of the press conference. The first was that Bryan Robson, on top of his toe, had now done his Achilles in as well.

And the second was Bobby Robson on Paul Gascoigne: 'He was the best player on the pitch – outstanding. He needs a bit more education, there's a slight over-exuberance – but his contribution was . . . well, I've got to be careful here. But he played very, very well – he made things happen, and he worked prodigiously hard.'

The conference then fell apart in translingual confusion when a journalist from Cameroon enquired mysteriously of Robson, 'Sir – you have said that Barnes and Waddle are the best pistons in the world.'

There's no answer to that.

I left the stadium around midnight and got a ride on the media bus into Rumourtown. At the station, the bedless rump were penned in the concourse with a major police presence, all riot gear and flashing lights again. I tried to sift from fans some picture of what had happened on the march.

People put the numbers from one to two thousand; and the numbers of those who went at the police, when they came on the roadblock, at one to two hundred. One fan spoke of a small group of police up a sidestreet getting 'a fearful pelting'; one police car was surrounded, and another one abandoned by its occupants, who fled.

But, people said, the people wanting trouble weren't ever going to stay ahead of that lot for long. The police regrouped, and came in from all sides; tear gas, rifle butts, batons. Fans trying to get away spoke of frightening crushes in the hallways of apartment blocks, or in garden areas against collapsing fences. One showed me welts and bruises on his arms and back from a beating he thought 'would never end'; another said he saw a girl get a caning, and her hand getting smashed.

And you came away with these questions:

Innocent or not – if you go among people who lob half-bricks at the *carabinieri*, what d'you expect but a beating?

Que sera sera
Whatever will be will be
We're going to I-tal-ee

Fine – but why d'you have to go *in a regiment*? Why d'you have to march?

Assertion, obviously. Then there's others who say (being fearful in an alien land, and short of the old cultural capital) that there's safety in numbers.

But that's a sorry delusion – no one got whacked for going to the stadium in twos and threes. The last thing the police were going to fancy was the lot of you together – whether it made you feel big or not, safe or not.

And why d'you have to feel big anyhow? Aren't you big enough on your own?

I hung around, among Sards doing likewise, watching nothing much happen at the station. A guy from BBC Radio told me how, in Stockholm, he interviewed a fan who seemed the acme of reason and plausibility. Half an hour later, he saw him carrying away his looted stash of brand new bowler hats.

*

The essence of what happened in Cagliari on 16 June is that – again – a small number of yobs got a large number of others mixed up in an upheaval; and it grew larger (albeit fairly briefly) than it need have done because, trembling with hooligan psychosis, the Italian security forces violently overreacted.

What did *not* happen is this:

> WORLD WAR!
>
> Rampaging English soccer thugs turned the streets of Sardinia into a bloodbath last night . . .
>
> More than 500 Brits were arrested . . .
>
> It happened after 1,000 angry fans hurled rocks . . .
>
> The arrested yobs – many of them drug-crazed . . .
>
> – *News of the World*

Les Walker, the FA's security man, later told me he estimated the number of hardcore trouble makers at around sixty.

Kay Coombes at the rotter conference the next morning reported five arrests.

The figure of seven English injured was confirmed; it was also thought that five police had been injured.

Moynihan made a statement: 'Orchestrated incident . . . minority of English thugs bring English football into disrepute . . . grateful to the police for swift and tough action.'

'I understand,' someone said, 'that things went well in Genoa last night.'

'Very well,' said a Scottish journalist. 'Jim Leighton made a save.'

John Williams muttered that the arrest figures were small 'because arrest isn't the agenda here. People don't get arrested – they get hurt.'

Brewin, Beauchampe, and Tummin of the FSA took the floor – another sign of the co-operation now beginning to get in gear, that the embassy gave them this facility to put over their views. The co-operation did not, however, go as far as they wanted – Moynihan had refused to meet them. (Unlike Dennis Howell.)

Brewin said the FSA totally condemned the forty or so English who threw rocks, etc.; and that they'd tried to stop the march. But they were, he said, extremely angry about the policing; and totally rejected Moynihan's hasty and ill-considered statement. Does he care, he asked, how people are being treated?

It then emerged, with some embarrassment, that the shit-stirring myth-maker Chris Wright, the self-styled 'organiser' of the march, was an FSA member, elected (unopposed) to their admin committee. He'd phoned Beauchampe and said, if the police threw a roadblock, 'the lads will smash right through it. If they want a confrontation they will get it.'

Brewin said they'd have to check their constitution – but that Wright wouldn't be a member of the FSA much longer. He was, they said, a compulsive liar, and a lonely man – always talking about the lads this, the lads that – and always turning up on his own, entirely ladless.

Then John Tummin gave his account of the evening's events.

He'd left the FSA office at five to six, joined the march, and moved up towards the front distributing copies of their guidebook. There was, at the front, a certain amount of aggression.

When they got to the junction of Viale Cimitero and Viale Armando Diaz, there were maybe forty or more Dutch fans ahead of them on the steps of the big church, the Santuario di Bonaria; police vans blocked the way, to prevent the English getting to those people.

There were two things wrong at this point. Firstly, the Viale Cristoforo Colombo, fifty or a hundred yards south, was broader, unoccupied, went directly to the stadium, and would have been a better, more segregated route.

And secondly, stopping people at a place where you had wasteground strewn with potential missiles to one side, and a half-dug-up pavement ditto to the other, was dim. (Les Walker agreed later – he put it tactfully – that the English police would have handled things rather differently.)

Some fans, said Tummin – he put it at between ten and thirty at this stage – now started throwing stones. The instant resort to tear gas in reply was, he said terrible policing – there was no graded response. They simply upped the stakes immediately, and induced panic and confusion among 1,500 people.

The police charged forward; he saw three *carabinieri* baton-beating a fan on the ground. He was with a group several hundred strong trying to get away, and find a different and safe way to the stadium; he saw three baton charges during this period. There were, he said, hundreds of people running scared and exhausted.

As he told the story, his re-living of it now became – understandably – emotional. He was also shaking a little.

The group he was with was charged again, and hotly pursued into a garage forecourt. He was hit several times by a policeman with a baton. There were now several hundred people crushed into a very small area on the forecourt. They were, he said, utterly terrified, jammed against a wall and a fence. People called in alarm, 'No Hillsborough – No Hillsborough.'

He was hit again. He showed an ugly bruising welt on his upper left arm.

The assistant deputy of the Cagliari police then arrived, one Antonio Pitea. Tummin had met him some weeks back, when they'd been trying to organise things for fans to do in Cagliari. He'd seen him also just a couple of days ago in the street; they'd shaken hands. Now Pitea, he said, came on to the forecourt, recognised him, said, '*Tu*' – and slapped him in the face.

He said, 'I've never seen a crowd so intimidated in my life. I was sitting on someone who was sitting on someone else, it was that crushed.' People were still being hit; people were dragged out and beaten right in front of them. 'People were impotent, they were crawling on their knees.'

No one was allowed to stand; eventually, Tummin was. It took some time to get it calm, and improvise a system to get people away. Then they were let out one by one; they were thoroughly searched, and taken in groups of twenty to the stadium.

It was, Tummin said, counter-productive, and might well prove a prelude or catalyst to more violence later. He characterised one of the later police charges in particular as 'a revenge attack'. Behaviour like this was, he said, only storing up trouble for the mainland; if anyone called policing like that a success, they needed their head looking at.

In the remaining days in Cagliari, I heard a number of tributes from fans – some unsolicited – to Tummin's courage and presence of mind at that garage. People said he had, simply, 'saved their hides'.

So I say sincerely, long may Tummin and the FSA prosper – but I also came away from this conference thinking they'll prosper more if they adopt a less confrontational public posture towards the various authorities that they feel are ignoring them, or worse.

For example: horrific though Tummin's experience may have been, calling the policing 'South African' (several times) is over-emotive, and not media-wise at all. They can lock you in the leftie cupboard easy with that sort of stuff – when what the hoolie trouble needs, more than anything, is perspective.

After all, you think England fans have problems? What about the fifty or so Romanian fans who had by now, in the light of events in Bucharest, applied for political asylum? *There's* problems . . . as for 'South African', frankly, my arse. Were they driving Caspars round and firing shotguns at you, John?

And then, how many people really were chucking rocks? The FSA says forty, Les Walker says sixty. The fans say one to two hundred . . . and the *News of the World* says a thousand.

The 23-year-old travel agent from Essex who'd been to Katowice – he'd been on the march too. When I met him three days later, he told it like this:

'It was the biggest mob I've seen outside of England–Scotland in Glasgow. There probably weren't even a hundred real hardcore at the front, actually hand-to-hand fighting – but there were more just cheering, yelling, running, chucking stuff. I mean, most people were in the mob 'cos it's a mob, not doing anything, just running back and forth – just in a mob, it's hard to say why you do it.

'The police stopped us 'cos there were Dutch down the road, but that's stupid, I've been against Dutch before and they're no trouble, they just come for the football, painted faces and that, they're fine, they're fun – they leave their bad ones at home. The papers whip it up, they're making bombs, all that – it's rubbish.

'Still, it was maybe forty minutes of trouble back and forth

– then they come at us from two sides and press us in this garage, they knew what they were doing – they had the helicopter up above. And that was panic, real panic, terrifying, we were crushed in there, hundreds of us, and the people coming at us were your real top nutters, your Italian SPG or whatever – but they'd taken a pelting, hadn't they?

'So you can't complain about police brutality – you can't give it, and not expect it back. I got big long bruises all over my arms and my back, but I was lucky, I only got the truncheons – it was the rifle butts that hurt – but they were bloody angry, it was frightening, the looks on their faces . . . if you lifted your face up it was whack, whack, whack. You had the choice, get crushed, or face the police – probably safer to face the police, it was like Heysel, piles of bodies . . . but you can't blame the police. I've got to be honest, you just can't. You're in their country, you've had a go at them, and that's that.'

He said, 'I don't believe it when they say it's just a minority. There's a majority who don't *come* for the trouble – but if there's trouble they'll join it all right. You can talk about it till you're blue in the face, but it's not a minority *once it's started* – because of the age group. You go down that campsite, it's all eighteen to twenty-five.'

He'd left the Pula campsite and come into town – spending more money in one day than in the whole nine days previous, on a cab and a room at the Italia – because, 'It was like a PoW camp, I was going mental out there. You've got Italians chucking acid at people, English staggering round pissed at four in the morning with knives – I'd had enough. I'm not running the actual camp down, the owner was brilliant, really looked after us, we had a whip-round for him – but it's just a mess out there.'

Then he said, 'There's less and less England going – look at it here. There's twice as many Scots, twice as many Irish. And like, I went for a beer last night (during the Italy–Czechoslovakia game) and all these birds walk in, and they've got their faces painted green, red, and white, and they're wearing green, red, and white dresses . . . you can't imagine the girls back home sitting watching in the pub with the George Cross on their faces, can you?'

England – just no fun any more.

In Genoa, the Scots marched to the stadium behind a forty-piece pipe band, and took the Swedes along with them. Not one Scot was arrested. They were even knocking on people's doors to introduce themselves – because when others get together, it's a party. But when the English get together, it's like a colonial land grab: the fag end of history, all played out . . . and if you're ugly and stupid, and you mass together looking that way, then you will – willingly or not – end up in ugly and stupid events.

The travel agent had done Sweden, Poland, Hungary, Romania, Spain, Denmark, and Greece ('wouldn't go there again'). For Mexico '86, he saved up for two years; he said, 'Mexico was so much better than here – it was such an achievement. Arriving at Acapulco was one of the best moments of my life – this rich American playground, and suddenly it's full of England fans. It's all tourism now, but it wasn't so much four years ago . . . and I did Germany too – we love Germany, they're so like us.

'But it wasn't a good time – same as here, same old thing – gets boring, sleeping at stations, and them coming in with the tear gas. It's not a break – my holidays every year are with England, and you come back more knackered than when you left. I mean, every time, you say never again – then you go again anyway.

'But it's getting frightening. I mean, someone's going to die – someone's going to die soon.'

I went from the rotter conference to the bus station, and found that the bus I'd used for Is Molas before didn't run on a Sunday.

Outside, three or four English were arguing with a taxi driver. One wore a T-shirt which said on the back, 'England's Finest – Invasion Of Italy 1990 – We Came, We Saw, We Kicked Ass'. On the front it said, 'The Nightmare Returns' over a picture of a bulldog bursting through a wooden wall, like Freddy on Elm Street.

Their idea of negotiating involved shouting and swearing a lot.

The driver took me to Is Molas for near half what he'd been asking of the fans to go to Pula – same distance, give or take. He said, on the way, that England were great, should have won 5–0. Butcher, he said, displayed 'a marvellous hostility'. Terry liked that.

His Italian was coming on. He tested his latest on his new mate the barman, grinning, '*Posso avere uno pompino*?'

It was a new word on me – I tried to think of *pomp-* words. Can I have a grapefruit? A fireman? An Argentinian goalkeeper? Seemed unlikely . . .

'A blow job,' Butcher laughed; his buddy the barman laughed happily with him.

They were chuffed over the way they'd played; but it was beginning to get boring, stuck in that hotel. You trained an hour and a half a day – then what? They'd been in Sardinia twenty-three days now . . . you entertained yourself as best you could. Ireland were playing Egypt in Palermo at five that afternoon – but no one expected that to be much of an entertainment.

I'd gone to see Peter Shilton. He'd won his 100th cap against Holland two years ago in Germany – not a nice way to get your century, watching Van Basten put a hat-trick past you. But last night, against Holland once more, he'd made a far greater milestone – his 120th cap took him past the Northern Irish keeper Pat Jennings to become the most capped international footballer of all time . . . but he wasn't thinking about that much, not now – not yet. He was still thinking about the game, and then the next one. Records, he said, are there for when you finish – on the night, you just want the result.

He said, 'It was a game where I didn't have a lot of work to do, not spectacular work – but it was difficult work, a lot of corners, and shots you expected to save. With it being 0–0, the worst period really was ten minutes to go. We tired a bit, and they were pushing on quite strongly from midfield; I just had the feeling we might give something away. That's when I was really working, shouting, because after all the good work we'd done, we hadn't finished them off – so the pressure was really on at the back not to let one in. From a personal point of view, even more so.'

I asked if he was satisfied, when it ended the way it did.

'I was satisfied with my own performance, very satisfied with a clean sheet, obviously – but I was a bit disappointed we hadn't won. We'd have more or less qualified if we had. As it stands now, we still need another result.'

And the Egyptians wouldn't be easy . . . he said, 'I made a complaint to FIFA about the pitch. The actual goalmouths, turf had been put in the goal, just in the six yard box, brand new turf. And it was coming away under your feet – not a big area, but you only need one slip there, it could be vital. You're trying to play in the World Cup . . . it was a disgrace. I couldn't believe the state of the goalmouths.'

He was rather more pleased about the fans. 'What impressed me about them was that the atmosphere was very jovial – it was a bit like you *normally* get abroad. There wasn't any bad chanting, or bad language, it was all good fun, good humoured – and they really got behind us. At the end the applause they gave us, it was great, I think they were really pleased with the way we played – and they're the ones that matter, aren't they? They kept singing, let's all have a disco, all that – it was fun. Quite unusual, really.'

So since we're talking unusual – how did it feel, to play behind a sweeper?

'Didn't affect me. At Derby, we played the last two games of the season with the same system, with Mark Wright sweeping – we beat Manchester City 1–0, then we played at Liverpool with it, and lost 1–0. Two of our best performances of the season – and Mark just slotted in, like he did last night. So it wasn't like we'd never done it – it was no problem.'

Then he said, 'As far as I'm concerned, I think all first division teams in England should play that way because it encourages players to think about the game, to make their own decisions. They have more space to create things, they have to play more. I think in England, this pushing up and playing in the middle third of the pitch, and the ball all helter-skelter – that's got to stop. It's not football. It's just tactical warfare, really – managers in England have got to open their eyes. The game is there to be *played* – it's not just picking up three points any old how, it's got to be played as an entertainment – and players have got to be encouraged to develop their abilities.'

But will it change?

'I think it's got to. I think if we do well here, that'll help. But there's one or two managers in England who've got to get the blinkers off and realise, their little world isn't the be-all and end-all of football. There's a big world out there, and we've got to be part of it.'

So would Shilton become a manager?

'I've got it in the back of my mind. Players I used to play with that are managers now, they all say, it's not bad on this side, but you play as long as you can. Because at the end of the day, playing's the best thing.'

Chris Waddle

The Man from Marseilles (with live commentary by Gazza and Barnesy)

If he weren't playing football . . .

'Still be working in the sausage factory, I suppose. I couldn't see me getting out of that – I didn't have the qualifications to move from there. I only knew football, and I was lucky enough to get into it – but I didn't get the break till I was nineteen. Everybody thought I was a bit small – then I got to eighteen and filled out a bit, played a season in the Northern League, and Newcastle gave me a year's contract. I'm twenty-nine now . . . Gazza. Sod off.'

We were sitting on the lawn at Burnham Beeches; the squad had been named, it was the eve of the Uruguay game, and Gazza was chucking grapes at us.

Waddle hadn't thought much about what he might do when the time came to come home from Marseilles. He said, 'If it means dropping divisions, I'll drop divisions, but I want to keep playing – I still get a thrill out of it. And people say when you pack it in, you really miss it.'

When he did pack it in, would he stay in the game?

'It's the only thing I really know. I love watching football, I love the tactical side of it, and I've had good managers – so I'd like to think some day I could put my ideas back into the game, maybe coaching, or scouting. I'd like to stay in it, anyway.'

So I asked about the managers.

'Arthur Cox at Newcastle, I've got great respect for him. I was nineteen, just arrived from Tow Law, and he was strong on discipline; I needed that. And he got me to believe – he thought I had something, and he was determined to make sure I didn't waste it. Then Terry Venables helped me at Spurs, he's got progressive ideas. I was sort of steady, going along, but I think with his ideas, it pushed me into another gear. I think he helped me a lot.'

And Bobby Robson?

'I think it's harder when you come to England, because all they can do is watch League games. And they expect you to do what you do for your club side – but international football's very different.'

'Bollocks,' said Gazza.

Waddle went on, 'I think being the England manager's all about motivating. It's up to the manager to get players to play with the confidence they have at their club – because when players get together here, it takes a while to feel part of it.'

Didn't he feel a part of it?

'Well, now I do – but it's took me a few years. Over the last year or more, I have done; before, I always felt a bit . . . why was I here, sort of thing. You look round and think, I remember watching them on the telly – they're England. And you don't feel as if you should be here with them. Some players, it's different . . . like Gazza here, he lacks a bit of confidence, doesn't he? Once he gets confident, God knows what'll happen.'

I asked how the two of them got on, with them both being Geordies.

'He was an apprentice when I was a pro, I had to beat him up then . . . yeah, we've known each other a few years.'

'Liar.'

'We've got the same ideas, he's just more stupid than me. When he come to Tottenham we had a good laugh, the last season I was there. So we've been the best of mates a while now – but deep down, I really hate him.'

'Cunt.'

I asked Gazza what he'd be doing, if he weren't playing football.

Waddle said, 'Throwing grapes at people.'

Gazza said, 'I've nothing to say.'

'If he hadn't gone for an apprenticeship at Newcastle, there were strong rumours he was going for an interview at the sausage factory . . . he's from a place called Dunston, and I'm from Pelaw, it's only five minutes in the car. And my wife, she's from a place about two minutes from where he lived.'

I asked, did it have any bearing on the way they played?

'I think up in Newcastle, everybody's brought up on the history of Newcastle United, the great players like Jackie Milburn, Bobby Mitchell, Terry Hibbett. Probably round the country all those people aren't legends – but in Newcastle they are. They've always had skilful players, like Jimmy Smith . . . in the north-east, people still talk about them.

'So when you're a kid, the first thing you do when you're on the park, you start dribbling the ball all the time. And it shows, in the England squad now – you've got myself, Gazza, Peter Beardsley, all from similar backgrounds, all skilful on the ball. So there must be something up there – you watch the young ones there, you'll always find there's two or three with exceptional skill. It's just getting them to believe, and play in a team pattern, that's the problem . . . at least, that's what they keep writing about us – saying we can do things, but that we don't play for the team, or that we haven't got defence. Well, we *haven't* got defence. But at the end of the day, the likes of Gazza, Peter and myself, John Barnes – we put bums on seats, don't we?'

Gazza said helpfully, 'Arses.'

'People say we haven't got defence, we don't do this, we don't do that – but if we can do the other thing . . . the other thing's harder to do than defend, anybody can defend. But my job's not to defend – yeah, you got to take your little part, so's Gazza, so's John Barnes. But what are we in the team for, really? To create, and to score. And if we're doing all right at that . . . I haven't got to prove it to anybody. Bobby Robson's the only one I've got to answer to when I'm playing for England. Nobody else.'

So what he said about playing in France the other night, after the Denmark game . . .

'4–4–2's the English system, has been for a long time. And some games it's fine, don't get me wrong, we'll pen teams in, and then I don't have to run back all the time. But when you're playing a class side, you end up defending a lot more. I've spoke to the manager about the times when their full backs keep creating, and I've got to go with them – and he says, That's just our system, you've got to do it. But it'd be great if I could just let them go, and find the space – so when we get the ball they could get it to me quick, and then *he's* out of position. It's all about bluffing then.'

He said, 'In Europe, they buy players to do a job . . .'

Gazza asked, 'Is he going to get paid for this?'

No.

'That's all he thinks about, Paul Gascoigne – *money*.'

Gazza laughed. He said, 'I'm money-daft.'

Waddle said, 'In Europe they buy players to do certain jobs – so I was bought to create goals for Papin, and it's worked out. Now there's certain games where I've had to run up and down, and I've spoke to the coach and said, when I get the ball at the other end I can't create, 'cos I'm going to have to run seventy yards. And he says, OK, we'll change it round . . . they're more flexible on the Continent. They'll change the system from game to game – but England, club sides as well, they'll play 4–4–2 from first game to last.'

So you come back and you think, This is dumb.

'Not *dumb*, no – but we've got a lot of quality players, and if we're wanting to get the best out of them . . . it's like Glenn Hoddle – if Glenn had been French he'd have played a hundred games, easy.'

Then Gazza broke in to say, 'Look at that little kid, look at him, watch.' There were kids in England shirts kicking a ball about by the net on the lawn; there often were, and Gazza'd always go to play with them, more than any other player. They loved it, always – and so did he.

Waddle looked at the kid and said, 'He's nineteen, man. He's got two paper rounds.'

Then he went on, 'People always say, why have we got to change? We had a good record in European football when we were in it, and the national team's gone seventeen without defeat. And they've got a point.'

But it was 2–1 to Uruguay the next day – and Waddle had a point too. 'I'm just saying we should be more flexible. Like, Denmark outnumbered us in certain parts of the field, and it was very hard to get the ball off them. I know it's hard to change the system, because as I say, we've done it all the time now – the only way we'd change it, to be perfectly honest, would be for whoever comes after the World Cup to say, right, I'm going to build a sweeper system . . . but I can't see it happening.'

That was interesting – Waddle assuming Robson would go (or be pushed) at the end of Italia '90. It was three days before the news of the job at PSV broke.

As to playing a sweeper, Robson was asked on the BBC the day after the Holland game, 'At what point did you take the decision to change the system so radically?'

He said, 'Oh, even before I came here. Before we set off.'

Back in the studio in London, Terry Venables looked ever so slightly dubious. He said, 'Well . . . if he had done, I'd have thought he'd have tried it before he'd gone. I think you like to look at what you're going to do.'

I said it was difficult for the national manager, when he was only getting the players a few days at a time.

'Yeah, but what I'm saying is, other teams look at the opposition and say, that's their strong point, let's outnumber them there – and they put players in to do that certain job. Then the flair players are left to go free – you look at the two Laudrups the other night, they didn't chase anybody, they didn't tackle anybody, they just found space to get the ball and create. So they must feel great when they get the ball, they feel fresh – and all of a sudden they're going at you. But when you run seventy yards up and down the right wing, it's very hard for ninety minutes . . . there might come a time in the last minute where you're one on one with someone – and you've got nothing left.'

So the English way stops you playing skilfully?

'It does at the finish, sure, because you get tired. Take him against Czechoslovakia – he had a blinding game, but the last ten minutes his socks went down, because he's done so much work.'

I asked Gazza if he'd been knackered at the end of that game. (Not so knackered that he couldn't score, though.)

'Nothing to say.'

Waddle laughed. 'Well, I don't know why his socks were down then.' Then he went on, 'In 4–4–2, the skill players play wide – but it's very hard to get the ball wide in international football.'

So against Brazil, I said, Waddle had come in.

'I had to. It was three on two in midfield, and I ended up just defending, I must have done more tackles than I've ever done in my life in that game. I was lucky I didn't get a yellow card at the finish, which is ridiculous for me . . . still, it's easy for me to say I should be playing here, or there – it's the English system, and you've got to take your part in it. It's just unfortunate that you have players like Glenn Hoddle, Stan Bowles, Frank Worthington, great technical players, the players people love to watch – and they can't hold a place in the England team.'

Then he said, 'This season, the greatest thing for me in English football has been Swindon. I've watched them play twice now. And we were in the north-east the other day and we said, what was it like with Newcastle in the Second Division? And everybody said – this is Newcastle supporters, mind – oh, Swindon were different class. And the players too, after the match, they said, oh, Swindon were different class. And why? Because he lets them play.'

'He' being Swindon's manager Ozzie Ardiles, previously one of the most attractive players Argentinian football ever produced – yet the FA wouldn't even give him a coaching badge. Then Swindon, having won promotion to the first division, were demoted to the third, for alleged under-the-table payments to players – without details of the charges being made public. A different club, one feels – one that wasn't different class – might not have been so swingeingly punished.

So was the extremity of the punishment revenge for Ardiles being foreign, and playing fancy, and winning? Given the xenophobic greedheads and dunderwits who run the English Football League, it's a suspicion that's very hard to avoid.

The FA's board of appeal, to their credit, subsequently eased Swindon's grief by putting them back into the second division – but what a dim and cack-handed affair it all was. And do ninety-one other clubs all have squeaky-clean hands?

Waddle said to Gazza, 'What are you sitting here for anyway? Haven't you got anything better to do than just follow me around?'

Gazza was chucking grapes in new directions now, and told Waddle to shut up; he was disturbing his aim.

I asked Gazza why he wouldn't talk to the press.

''Cos I fuckin' hate them.'

Waddle said, 'I don't blame him, actually. He's got his

contract with the *Sun*, so he only speaks to one journalist, and he just blanks the rest. Fair enough.'

Later, in Cagliari, when the press–squad relationship was hitting its nadir, I asked Butcher if everyone going round saying they hated the press, but still taking money from them, wasn't a bit . . .

'Hypocritical? Yeah, well – the *Star* was very derogatory towards me, and I'm contracted to them, so I said, right, contract's over. But then, I could legally have fallen down by that – so I had to do more articles. And they're very positive articles, all my articles have been positive – but that only shows how today's news is tomorrow's fish'n'chip paper.'

It's not a satisfactory answer. It's no good saying that when they're bad, they're very very bad – but that when they're paying and you give them decent stuff, it's here today, gone tomorrow.

So I said, given how bad it had got by then, shouldn't the players all just say, stop – no more contracts, no more interviews, no nothing.

'What, with the scandals and that? Yeah . . . but it's good money, at the end of the day, for fifteen minutes on the telephone. And you try to say positive things. If they want sensationalism, they can get someone else.'

But why do you have to be paid to be positive?

Another thing: when they criticise the press, it's blanket criticism.

But they can discriminate all right, when they justify their paid columns by saying the hack who's appointed to do them is OK. One player said his appointed scribbler was leaving his tabloid, he couldn't stick it any more – and that showed his integrity.

I'd just seen the hack in question buying blank receipts for cash from a Cagliari cabbie . . . very bloody integral.

But later, in Naples, Waddle gave a more honest answer to this criticism. He said, basically, that it was great taking money from people that you hated.

I asked what was it like to score a goal – and Gazza forgot his vows of silence immediately. He said, 'It's *brilliant*.'

'D'you want to take this interview over? Well shut your

face then.' Answering the question, Waddle said, 'It's a great feeling. For ten seconds, you just lose your head.'

'It's unbelievable,' said Gazza, 'you feel like shooting your bolt.'

'You do? I never went that far.'

Gazza was caught up in the magic idea now. 'You're all over the place, all over the place, man. Run anywhere. Even if you're 5–0 down.'

'Aren't you slightly exaggerating there?'

I said to Gazza, he was a confident player, so . . .

Down came the clamp again. 'Nothing to say.'

'You'll get nothing off him.'

Someone else told Gazza he should say, no comment, like a politician.

'You don't say, no comment. Then they can put that you said, no comment. But if you say, I've got nothing to say . . .'

'They'll put that you said so.'

Gazza sat there shrugging.

Waddle went back to goals. He said, 'You can't explain the feeling, everything just goes out your head for ten seconds, it's just jubilation – me personally, I'll always sprint for ten, twenty yards when I score. I'll never walk away. I just seem to run and go stupid for ten seconds. At Marseilles, everybody who scores jumps the barrier and goes to the fence, and I'm like that too – in England, you've got to watch that, you might be provoking trouble, but in France you don't. They love their football there – and then, you like to see people go home happy. They go to work or school on Monday, and they talk about it. If you can entertain people like that, it's fantastic.'

Gazza by then had gone to kick the ball about with the kids on the lawn. And he was fooling about – he was entertaining.

Waddle said, 'You either love him or you hate him – but you'll find most people love him. He's cheeky, but he gets away with it – he's got one of them faces. And the way he says things, it always sounds like he's playing funny – but sometimes he's serious.'

I said how everyone joked that Gazza had a confidence problem – and that maybe, on the park, he was that confident. But mightn't he act the way he did because, inside, he wasn't really so sure of himself at all? Terry Venables has said he's a sensitive boy . . .

Waddle said, 'People like that are normally a bit insecure, even when things are going for them. They like to be the centre of attraction, and feel wanted. And maybe with Gazza that might be it.'

But whatever it is with Gazza, he's not telling unless you pay; I'm not sure if he'd know how or what to tell anyhow, however much you paid. And so long as it keeps him playing the way he does, I doubt also whether there's many who'd complain.

'They don't realize you're a foreigner, that you can't speak the language, and you need help. To be fair, Marseilles, they're like the most powerful thing in the city – if the club rings the electricity and says, I want electricity for Chris Waddle, then *boom*, you've got it. Whereas if I ring up, it probably takes a few days, you're on a list, a week or two goes by . . . at the finish I had to say, look, you don't do anything for us, I need electricity, I got problems – and maybe that's partly why I'm not doing so well on the field as early as I wanted – then all of a sudden, the next day the electricity arrives, and the day after that the phone . . . nine times out of ten a club signs you and says, right, get on with it. And if it's an English club fair enough, you haven't got a language problem – but going abroad, it was a nightmare at first. I thought, what the hell am I doing here?'

I asked if he was learning the language.

'Yeah, I've had quite a few lessons now. But because I've been playing Saturday, Wednesday, Saturday a lot, League and Cup, I've not always had time. All of a sudden the teacher'll knock, like, the night after a big game, and the last thing you want is to sit down and learn French. So I've missed out a few – but my wife's stuck at it, she's ahead of me now. Still, I get by – I'm not as good as her, I'll never speak perfect, I end up trying to speak a sentence, and an English word falls in it. But I'm having a go – the lads reckon another year, and I'll be able to speak pretty good.'

And certainly, he was enjoying it enough now – on and off the pitch – that he wanted to stay. He lives up the road from Marseilles in Aix-en-Provence in a rented house; and he talks about it like Lineker did about Barcelona – great people, great food, great weather. He's got a two-year-old daughter who's enjoying it too – she's in the pool every day. He said, by the time the contract finished, if he stayed, she'd be five, and growing up bilingual. It was an idea he liked.

'But then I mean, Marseilles – you get the impression that if you don't do it, you'll not be there. You've got to think, I'm a foreign player, I'm not a French player – and there's only three foreigners allowed. So if he gets his eye on one he wants . . .'

Marseilles had on its books that season Chris Waddle, the Uruguayan Enzo Francescoli, and the Brazilian Mozer.

'At the minute I'm in a strong position, I know I'll not be going. I get on well with the public, I like the spectators over there . . .'

After Italia '90, Marseilles's owner Bernard Tapie sold Francescoli to, funnily enough, the newly promoted Cagliari; and replaced him with Dragan Stojkovic, from Red Star Belgrade. Seeing as he was buying Adidas at the time, swapping a couple of footballers around probably didn't exercise him too much.

I asked Waddle about the money players make.

'You get great rewards – why not? It's a short life. And I'm lucky, I know – well, people say footballers are lucky, but you work hard too. And if that means going to a big club, and playing for England, it's not just luck, is it? If Baggio, say, goes for eight million or whatever, good luck to the lad, he's secure for life, good luck to him – because he's got pressure on him, hasn't he? Especially in Italy. I mean, I was flattered that Marseilles went so high for me – but we've won the League, got to the semi-final of the European Cup and got robbed in it . . .'

What happened?

'We won 2–1 at our place – so we went to Benfica, and if they won 1–0 it was theirs, with the away goal. So it was 0–0, seven minutes to go, the cross come in – and the kid's punched it in the net. It was blatant, everybody saw it.'

Except the referee.

'Unfortunately, yes. That's why I said after the match there – I didn't mean to slag him off, he's under enormous pressure, there's 110,000 there – but it's about time for big games, and all World Cup games, that they have the video replay, like they have in American football. Because for the time it takes to rewind and have a look, after all . . .'

There'd have been no hand of God in Mexico then – or, indeed, in Naples against the Russians.

'Yeah, well, if they'd looked at that, they'd have said no. And I mean, be fair – the player who does that, and then runs away giving it all this (he mimicked the exultation of the scorer), they should send him off – he's just conning the game. How Maradona can say it's the hand of God – it's the biggest load of crap I've ever heard. If he'd have come out after the match and said, yeah, I handled it – everybody would have thought, well, at least he's honest. 'Cos at the end of the day, if Gary Lineker had done the same everybody here might have said, well done – but Gary would have said, I handled it. I would have. And what annoys you is Maradona always says, he didn't handle it – what, is he frightened to admit he did?'

He said, 'There's Gazza, obviously – but I've never really been one to mix with the players off the field. You tend to go with your own friends. Obviously I've drifted away a bit, not being in Newcastle any more . . .'

I asked, was it hard to stay close to people, when you started in a sausage factory, and ended up in Marseilles?

'I know what you mean. I had a row with one of my mates once 'cos he said, it's all right for you, you get the privileges – I remember one night I was in this social club in Pelaw, and me and this lad carried on, and he ended up getting barred, and I didn't. And then his brother come up one night, he's talking to me, and all of a sudden he's just let himself go, he says, it's a joke our kid's barred, and you're not, just because you're Chris Waddle. At the time I thought, that's stupid, we both carried on but he got caught, they thought he was causing trouble more than I was. But then you realise, you do get the privileges – but that's just football, because everybody loves the game. So you do get better treatment.'

And it has its downside.

'Sometimes you don't know people's true personality, they come on false with you 'cos of who you are. There's people want bits of you – everybody's out for something. I'd like to think I've spotted the ones that are just hangers-on – but there's a lot who don't. They don't realise it's the club these people love, or the game, not you – and when you move, say, they don't give a shit about you any more. Or a new player arrives, and they leech on to him instead. At first it starts, oh, you're a great player, fancy a drink, have a drink, blah blah blah – and within a month it's, can you get us a ticket? So you go sure, good mate, I'll get him a ticket. And all of a sudden it's a ticket every game. Then they winkle their way into the club, and they start mixing with all the players, and they love it, that's what their dreams are about – not you.'

In Marseilles, he said, the people were great, sure – but there'd always be people, say, wanting him to go to their restaurant. 'And I know what they're after – they're not after Chris Waddle, they wouldn't have time to get to know what I'm like – it's just Chris Waddle, Olympic Marseilles. Not me. And you have to be careful not to be rude all the time. You have to keep saying, no, sorry – you want to get home, and see your family.'

Was it more tempting, when he was younger?

'Oh yeah. I mean, the friends I was knocking about with, they were on the dole – and all of a sudden I'm on the first team, my money's going up, and there's people offering you free this, free that, free driving lessons . . . OK, great. And then all of a sudden I'm in a car now, I've bought an old banger, I got an old Capri for £100. So I can take my mates out during the day – and for a few months, 'cos my missus was working, I used to just drive around . . . well, wasting money, probably. But at the time, that was what I wanted to do. I didn't really grow up till I went to Tottenham.'

He said, 'Who's going to stand and get kicked? People say, look at him jumping out the way – but it's not being a coward, it's just using your loaf. In France, you can see a lot of it coming. Brest, they were pulling us, tripping us – they beat us 2–1, maybe to them that was the best way of getting the result. We ended up trying to fight them – and that's not what we're best at.'

He said he'd never been sent off; he'd been booked once in France, and four or five times in England.

'I can't get physical – I'm not going to launch into people

and smash them in half. My bookings have been obstruction, maybe, or telling the ref where to go . . . I like to talk to the ref. If I think his decisions are crap, I'll say so. I got booked once at Newcastle, when I first went back with Tottenham. We were getting beat 2–1 – and he give some stupid decision and I just said, that's a load of crap. So he gives me the yellow card, in front of the Newcastle fans . . . I suppose they liked it. I didn't.'

He said he approached games pretty relaxed, generally. 'People say, look at him, sauntering out – what do they want, they want veins popping out my neck? In our changing room, there's only really Terry who's like that. He's all, *yeah, come on, come on* – but it'd look a bit funny if everyone was like that, wouldn't it?'

'Marseilles happened so quick. We were in Cyprus, and I was talking about the next season, playing with Gazza, and Gary Lineker coming – I was looking forward to it, I thought, this is what we need, a world class goalscorer. Then we get back – and two weeks later we're in Marseilles. It happened so quick, it was just so quick – bang bang crash bang wallop, I was there.'

What would he have done if his wife had said no?

'I wouldn't have gone. The first three months, there were times when I wish I'd said no myself. But I wouldn't change it now – it was a real challenge. Then after Marseilles people say, what you going to do? And I'd like another challenge – probably with a second division club. You look at the big old clubs, Burnley, Blackpool – it'd be nice to see if the support would come back, like when Kevin Keegan went to Newcastle. That must have been a great thing to do. He must have known he could get thirty thousand in there – and he did.'

Then he remembered George Best coming to play against Newcastle, and watching standing in the Paddock, and 10,000 being locked out. He talked about skill players all the time; and he said he always liked playing against the Italians, club or country, because, 'They've got the technique, haven't they? They draw you in, they try to get you nearer goal – but that suits my game. You get into the sort of zones where it's hard to get into, and all of a sudden you're there with ease – and you think, I'm enjoying this.'

Was he a better player then, for playing abroad?

'I feel better, yeah. But it's hard to show you're a better player in the system here – for me to show I'm better, we'd have to play like Marseilles. 4–4–2, it's hard to express yourself.'

We were sat inside with a cup of tea; John Barnes crept up and leant through the window, mock-throttled Waddle from behind, then came in – rolling through the window – to snaffle our biscuits.

Waddle said, 'He's in the same position as me. You get a marker, and you've got a zone – so you haven't got the greatest amount of space to get rid of him. You've got to stick in your zone for the system – so sometimes the ball comes, and you've just got to pass it off. Then people say, oh, he doesn't dribble, he doesn't do what he's doing for Liverpool – but in international football, they're not daft. They say, he's dangerous, get tight on him. If he went wandering away with the ball, what would the bloke do then? If he went into the middle of the park, it's common sense that the full back should just go – but it doesn't work like that. We play such a zone system, you've all got your little areas . . . it must be great, marking a player who plays wide for England.'

'If you just stay out there,' said Barnes.

'But then if you go wandering, all of a sudden they're looking to get the ball out there, or the full back does stay back – and you're wrong, 'cos you've left your zone.'

'Also, Chris, I can play for Liverpool, and it's like the continentals – they'll have someone in that zone, but *not necessarily the same person.* So Alan Hansen can go past me, and I'll take his position. But here, if Chris comes off the line, or I come off the line, and no one goes into that position, if the full back doesn't come – then the marker's free. With the sweeper, the full back can go, and the sweeper can cover; or the marker can cover, and the sweeper can mark – you're not caught short anywhere. In England, they place too much importance on position – if you're midfield you're midfield, if you're a winger you're a winger. But a midfielder on the wing, he's not a midfielder any more, is he?'

'But because they're not used to it, they'll quickly run back . . .'

'To get to their position, yeah.'

'He could go on a run, or chase somebody, and end up over here – and instead of just saying, all right, I'm here now, you just stay there a couple of minutes until it's sorted out, then we'll swap back around – they don't, do they? They'll run straight back and say, no, no, I'm here, you've got to be there. And for the likes of him and me, it's very frustrating, because we're in the team to create, and do things. And if you can't get the ball, what are we in the team for? People write, we didn't really do anything – it's a load of crap, we work as hard as anybody else when we play those positions – but we're there to create, not defend. At Marseilles, if I lose the ball, I don't have to break my neck to get back – the manager says, you three don't worry about defence, the rest'll do that. And you're not going to tell me seven others and the goalie can't defend. How many defenders do you want? It's just *inflexible* – that's the difference between Europe and us. People go on about Liverpool – but they play near enough European . . .'

'That's why Liverpool have been successful. I wouldn't say they're *as* flexible as the European teams . . .'

'But they're more flexible than any other English team.'

'Yeah. Players rotate, they move around, they're difficult to mark – Glenn Hysen's created goals on the right wing, and is he that kind of a player? But he made two goals against Coventry; he's a centre-half and he ends up down the right, and one of the midfield players drops back . . .'

'It's just common sense.'

'In England you're happy marking your man. But all of a sudden if your man goes somewhere else, you're not happy. In Europe you'd go with him.'

'Because they know they've always a spare defender. So they rotate it amongst themselves – it's very simple. Whereas here, if he goes inside, and then the ball gets knocked out to their full back, nine times out of ten coach'll be out the dugout and it's, *what are you fuckin' doing in the middle of the park?*'

'And then Chris or myself'll have to run back with this full back. And we end up in the left back or right back position.'

'I'll tell you, when you play Liverpool – everybody goes out saying, how we going to stop them? He marks him, he marks him, he marks him – and they still come out winning two or three-nil. You think you do your homework – but they take you into positions which no other English club does.'

Waddle and McMahon later agreed, in Naples, that they'd back Liverpool to beat England two times out of three.

Anyone for 4–4–2?

Asked after the Holland game whether he could contemplate changing back to it for Egypt, Robson said, 'Sure, I could contemplate changing. I've only played it once, I've played eighty-nine times the other way . . . I could contemplate abandoning the sweeper system, yeah.'

I had more sympathy with Barnes now, in May, than I'd had with his more equivocal, stubbornly uncontroversial position at Anfield in April – Waddle's directness had brought him out. Even so, he did revert to the party line towards the end, saying with more hope than belief that we'd be OK . . . but not Waddle.

Waddle said that to be fair, the boss had let him off the leash in some games lately – saying that if he wasn't getting a kick, to come inside. He'd enjoyed Italy, and Yugoslavia.

But then he said, about the World Cup coming, 'Egypt, they'll be man-to-man. And if they mark man-to-man, like, where I go, he goes – then I'll say to the coach before the game, I'm not staying there, I'll go wander. Because I know he's not punishing my team – if they get the ball, he's still not going away from me. And why have I got to stay right wing, if I know this man's not going anywhere? Why right wing, instead of right *side*? It's a half of a half, isn't it?

'You cannot say, for the balance of the team – that's rubbish. That man's staying with me, so if I take him in, somebody's got to be spare somewhere. That's all I'm saying. It'd be nice, if I get a man-to-man marker in the World Cup, if he just said, OK, he's obsessed with you, he's not going to attack – so go where you want. Be flexible.'

That's what you're hoping for?

'I'm hoping.'

And he got what he hoped for, in the end – then proved what he could do with it too, when it turned out to be England who drew the task of mastering the Belgians. Waddle played the full 120 minutes in that game, and was one of the best things we had.

But sadly, John Barnes didn't, and wasn't. He had a good goal disallowed, which was bad luck, and he got a groin strain, which was worse – but he never showed out the way Chris Waddle did.

Changing the system doesn't work any automatic magic – it only helps you if you help yourself.

Stumbling Out of Cagliari

Bull, Platt, Barnes, and England–Egypt

While the gunmen of West Beirut celebrated Egypt's draw with the Irish by firing volleys into the Lebanese sky – joined, in a rare show of Arab solidarity, by Syrian troops, which just shows the barriers that football can surmount – Jack Charlton, as we know, was being less than courteous about their game.

The Egyptian manager Mahmoud El-Gohary politely refused to respond, and ordered silence from his players too. Dr Ahmed El-Mokadem, however, a professor of economics from Surrey University who was helping to fund Egypt's travel and accommodation, did not feel so constrained. Speaking to the *Independent*, he described the Irish way of playing as 'contagious crap'.

He said it wasn't only the Egyptians that the Irish fans booed after their 0–0 draw. 'They're fed up with not seeing good football. If that's the way their team's going to play every game, they'd prefer to be getting pissed in the pub.'

He also said, 'Our players get no match fee, no regular income from football, and have no insurance against serious injury. Would you believe our chaps are on $100 for a win here? Their bonuses are peanuts. You would spend it in an hour over the bar. That is the standard by which you must measure their achievement in drawing with Holland and Ireland.'

It was, indeed, no mean achievement – but then, like Robson had said, they had some very good players. In the run-up to Italia '90 they'd got draws against Denmark, South Korea, Austria, and Colombia – they'd beaten the Czechs, and they'd walloped the Scots 3–1 in Aberdeen.

And there weren't too many English in Sardinia who

reckoned getting out of Cagliari against this lot would be easy.

Group D sorted itself out at five in the afternoon of the 19th, though not entirely to form. Yugoslavia beat the UAE 4–1 in Bologna; but in Milan the Colombians held the Germans, until Littbarski scored in the 88th minute. It looked then as if predictions of their demise were accurate; but with the referee allowing four minutes of extra time for stoppages, after a game raddled with fouls and histrionics, Valderrama put Rincon through to equalise in the 92nd.

What, then, to make of these Colombians? They were daft, basically – Higuita made two 'saves' nearer the half-way line than his goal, using his feet and his head; while the outfield players (or, one should say, the *other* outfield players) were a volatile mix of lovely skill, crazy rough-house, and melodramatic mock-injury of truly Argentine proportions.

It had been the stereotype of African football that they were extravagantly skilled, and totally disorganised; but Egypt and Cameroon had scotched any patronising notions that the Africans were naive in this way. If anyone was 'African', on the contrary, it was these wacko Colombians – whose tactical formation, theoretically 4–4–2, could in despairing reality be best described only as 11. From Higuita onward, they popped up all over the park with a feckless, disconcerting, and anarchic abandon – and now they were through.

So in Milan and Bologna, there were parties.

Cagliari, on the other hand, was empty – the fans had scattered round the island to get away from the police. We were the morgue of the World Cup.

I ate at La Taverna, where the kindly owners always made me feel like ET: 'Have you phoned home?' Then I went back to the Italia, for the day's second bout of matches in Group A.

In Florence, the Austrians and the Americans kicked each other to a meaningless, tedious, foul-tempered 2–1 win for . . . well, it wasn't ever going to be the USA, was it?

Matters Roman were more weighty and more beautiful by far. The Italians played the Czechs to decide the winner of the group – a prize of huge import to the hosts, as the group winner stayed in Rome for the next round. But because the Czechs had run up five against the Americans, their goal difference meant a draw was enough – whereas the Italians had to win. Waking up after their American sleepwalk, they did so in style.

Salvatore 'Toto' Schillaci started for the first time, in place of Carnevale. And Vialli was injured – a frenzied debate began over whether the injury was real, or just the result in Vialli's head of not scoring any goals – but either way, it meant Roberto Baggio, at last, stepped up and started too.

The Italians went ahead in the ninth minute, Schillaci heading home for his second goal of the tournament – and they started playing the loveliest football we'd seen so far. Donadoni was electric, Giannini was everywhere, Baresi was masterful; altogether they were neat and fast, one man past another, dazzling and bewildering, graceful and inventive . . . yet *still* they couldn't convert it into goals. Two minutes after he'd scored, Schillaci missed Berti's cross by inches; then Baggio got through twice – and twice Stejskal saved.

So it was beautiful, yes – but when would they ever get deadly?

Baggio had such touch, such imagination – pass after pass released men into space, more often than not Schillaci, who kept racing through with fiery-eyed speed and acceleration. In the 54th minute, he was denied a clear penalty. Then an equally abominable decision at the other end denied the Czechs a perfectly good goal, for an offside that never was.

And it stayed at 1–0 – until Baggio scored unanswerably in the 77th, picking up the ball at the half-way line, beating two men, sending a defender the wrong way, stranding the keeper, and sliding it home. *That* was what Juventus paid near eight million for . . . and it looked like the Italians, at last, had found the dream team up front that they'd been waiting for. Italy 2, Czechoslovakia 0.

The junction of Via Roma and Largo Carlo Felice turned instantly into total hooting dementia. The freighters from Korea and Yugoslavia sat bright-lit at the dock; the tram lines overhead were a glistening net of electricity; and beneath them the cars surged and shoved, manically honking and parping, flags flying from every window, the scooter boys weaving through with their flags waving too – all watched by masses of people poured out from their houses all round town, and now standing on street corners and central reservations, chanting and shouting,

EE-TAL-YAH! EE-TAL-YAH!

Oh-laaaaay, oh-lay oh-lay oh-lay
Oh-lay, oh-oh-lay

It was maximum street party, no beer required. Helpless traffic cops meandered about grinning in the middle of the cacophanous jam; people sat on car roofs, hung out of windows, screamed from balconies.

It was a shame there were so few English left to enjoy it.

You know how it is – you go without sleep for a night, and it's basically OK. Then you sleep seven hours the next – and wake up feeling like a tree fell on your head . . .

I went to the press centre – this is the day before the game now – and there were still no tickets for England–Egypt. I came close to my first sense of humour failure since Florence in May. There was no discernible system yet for second round tickets either, though that began in Naples and Bari in only four days' time . . . but Olivetti, someone said, were bringing new machines. If so, great – new bugs, new glitches, new memory wipes . . .

Nottage was at the centre, looking fraught. Lately she'd been staying in town, at the Panorama; the man in the room next door woke her at 6.30 every morning, with alarm call regularity, by noisily vomiting.

We went out to the training ground, where knots of kids had been let in to gawp. Players, Butcher more than anyone, gave them time and talk, autographs, team photos and badges; he put his arm round people's shoulders for their snapshots, bending a bit so as not to make them look too tiny. You'd never know he'd been dropped.

The only person Butcher wasn't making happy was his contract man, the No. 2 from the *Star*. He'd been told he had to talk, so he was talking – but he wasn't saying anything.

Peter Beardsley, meanwhile, stood alone and apart by the Gatorade table. I always liked Beardsley; he was quiet and modest, and, when you finished talking with him, he always said thank you – which was almost absurdly courteous since, of course, it should have been you thanking him. But being a nice guy never got a man picked.

The biggest throng, as ever, was round Lineker – cameras, scribblers, fans. Even the police wanted autographs.

Robson did the BBC, Sky, and a Mexican crew. Then it was the English press, with the Italian press waiting.

Item one on the agenda was the state of Lineker's toe – they'd been drilling it and draining it, getting out the blood from under the nail . . . yeeucch. He couldn't put his foot in his boot; he wasn't training. 'But,' said Robson, 'we haven't got another Gary Lineker.' It would, if necessary, be a painkilling injection, and out you go anyway.

Bryan Robson's toe, on the other hand, was 'responding' – but his Achilles wasn't. The manager was planning the team without him.

'Who's taking over the captaincy?'

Silence – then laughter.

'You'd have caught me eight years ago. Not now.'

Someone probed, suggesting the selection was bound to disappoint a few.

'It'll disappoint eleven. The players know the team. So if it gets out now, we'll know one of them talked.'

Of the Egyptians he said, 'We think we're due a goal, and we think they're due to concede one. If we get in front we'll be OK – but they have one or two that need looking after. If he gets a draw he'll be satisfied – but I won't be. We need our boys to be world class, not club class. Some threaten, some deliver . . . I wish the skipper was in, I'll tell you.'

At which point it emerged that Bryan Robson had, at his own expense, flown a faith-healer over – one Olga Stringfellow – and also that the *Sun*, at their own expense, had sealed her off in the Exclusive zone.

The skipper, said Robson, was convinced this woman got results. Three weeks before the Poland game last October, he'd had a stress fracture, it had been there on the X-ray. Then he saw this woman and *boom* – no more fracture.

Robson said the Doc and Fred Street would talk with her, and report back. 'But it's me who decides if he's fit. I'll say to him, right, show me. Sprint like hell fifty yards, brake, turn – do that for fifteen minutes.'

Otherwise, he said, faith-healers – it was no story, it was irrelevant. 'What I've been through the last eight years, I'd have needed three thousand of them. One wouldn't be enough, he'd be worn out. Still, the skipper believes it works – how, I don't know. And he's doing it with our knowledge.'

Would Robson himself go to talk with her?

He said, to roars of knowing laughter, '*I'm* not going in her room – and that's off the record. If it comes up, you'll have me down the corridors with a machine gun.' Then he said, 'All right, lads, that's it – and let's keep it to football, shall we? Anybody doesn't, I'll wrap a chair round his head.'

He started to get up – but then Nottage reminded him, there was still the Italian press to talk to.

'Awww nnn . . . yes. OK.'

And round and round we went, all over again.

'To lose to Egypt is unthinkable for us.'

'Like losing to the USA in 1950?

'That's forty years ago – but it would be similar. So I'll play eleven goalkeepers.'

When it was over, Robson went off for a spin in a Tornado from the NATO base down the road. And that at least, one imagines, would clear the worries from the mind, just for a Mach 1 moment or two.

At Is Molas, I learnt of COL people selling their tickets for the Final at £500 apiece . . .

At the bar, Butcher's Italian was coming on; he'd progressed from fellatio to cunnilingus.

Then, as I sat down to talk with Steve Bull, Lineker came in to shake his hand, and congratulate him.

So there was one of Robson's key selections for Egypt. Steve Bull – who'd come on eight times for England, six times as a substitute, and, remarkably, had already scored four goals – was now to start his first competitive international.

Robson had said about him going on against the Dutch, 'Bully found himself in a match out of all proportion to anything he's ever been in in his life. In all his life.' And he came close twice then, too . . .

So I asked – my favourite question – what Stevie Bull would be doing, if he wasn't there, and playing football.

'Couldn't tell you. Last job I had was in a builder's yard, so I'd probably still be there now.'

He'd had an operation on a knee when he was seventeen, and they said he'd never play again – but three weeks later, he was back on the park. He played with a local team, Tipton Town – and when he was eighteen, a scout from the Albion took him there for training, a couple of times a week.

'I thought I'd gone past it by then, eighteen, you know – schoolkids nowadays come in sixteen, fourteen – I thought I'd got no chance. But it suddenly kicked off. They had me on a three month trial, and after a month I'd scored twelve goals, something like that – so they give me a one year contract. Then Ron Saunders had me in one day, he says, somebody's come in for you. And I says, who? – and it's Wolves. I thought, oh – I thought I'd got a future at the Albion, like, I'd had four games, and scored two goals; I thought I had a chance there. But he made it clear it wasn't worth stopping any more, so it was signed and sealed that day. And I've had four years there since – enjoyed every minute.'

He was twenty-five now; and had built up a degree of faith among his fans in his abilities as a goal machine that even Olga Stringfellow would envy. I asked how it felt to be sat on the bench at Wembley and have people screaming through the wire at Bobby Robson to put him on.

'It's a bit embarrassing sometimes. I can't get on there and score goals all the time – they're chanting for me, then I might go out and have a nightmare. But I enjoy it, I enjoy all the publicity, all the stuff in the papers. You can never stop them cheering for you, can you? That's what gets you on the pitch.'

What about when people criticised his first touch – or, more bluntly, just said he didn't have one?

'I think that's a load of rubbish, myself. Everybody has bad first touches – it's on the day, isn't it? Not being bigheaded or anything, but I think I've got as good a first touch as anybody else. You can never stop learning, though – not being disrespectful to Wolves, but it's nice being here, seeing different class players. The more skilful players, Peter Beardsley, Barnesy, all them – they've got touch everywhere, they're the gifted players – but then, I'm gifted with scoring goals.' He said, 'I'm just an old-fashioned target man, really. I just try and get my head and my foot in everywhere, and score goals.'

I asked what it was like, scoring.

'Unbelievable. Inside your body, it's like a tingling feeling – specially if it's for your country. My first goal against Scotland, I could have cried when I scored that goal, the feeling inside me . . . it's unbelievable.'

Gazza said it's like coming.

He laughed out loud. Then he said, 'It is, actually – like, aaawwwhhh . . . you're a bit drained after it. He's round the bend anyway – but it is a bit like that. A bit relieving.'

So I asked what it was like, playing with Gazza, and he laughed again; he said, 'He's a bit soft, but he's all right, he keeps the spirit going – and he's confident. You need someone just to steady him down, Pop Robson, or Steve McMahon, 'cos he's a bit wild in his head – but his skill is unbelievable, different class. The flicks, the touch, the tackles – it's just nice to watch the things he does. In training he's always practising, flicking it over his head, or whatever – he's always doing something.'

And how did he feel about starting tomorrow?

'Bit nervous. It's everybody's ambition, isn't it? People'd give their right leg to be where I am right now. But I'll just go out and enjoy it, I'll play my normal game. I'm nervous now, you're thinking up to it, you want to get started – the first ten minutes might be a bit nervy. But I'll get into it. I'll just play the way I always play.'

A journalist, I said, had fancied him against the Dutch, because he didn't reckon Koeman'd like some hairy-arsed skinhead charging up his backside . . .

But Bull only laughed again. 'If they want to put it like that, they can – but I'd have enjoyed going on from the start. When I went on for the last half-hour I had two chances, I should at least have put one of them away. So who knows what might have happened if I'd gone from the start? You get a bit of frustration, on the bench – you know you can get on there, you can do what you're good at. And when you see chances missing you think, ohhh God . . . but it's easy said when you're sitting down and watching it. I went on and had two chances, and there'll be other players thinking, oh Christ, look at that.'

I asked whether it wasn't a bit odd, going on for just a few minutes, like he had against the Irish.

'Yeah, it's a bit weird – but it's another cap, isn't it? One minute, two minutes, half-hour, it doesn't matter – it's another cap. You get a cap come through the post, another cap on the wall – it's a bit of pride, isn't it?'

And was it a whole different thing, going on against Holland in the World Cup?

'I've had nothing like it at all. The first experience was coming on against Scotland at Hampden, in front of 60,000 people – I enjoyed it, specially scoring as well . . . but coming on against Holland here, live on television – that's different altogether. I don't know how you can put it in words – Gullit, Rijkaard, all that . . . it's nice to be on there with players like them.'

What about all the media attention – how did he feel about that?

'They go a bit overboard – but I just let them get on with it, it's their job, they've got to do it. I've rung home and told them, but they know what the papers are like. I read them here, I see what they've put, and I think to myself, nah – I never said that. I don't know where they get it from.'

The way he said these things, Bull seemed as good and straight and simple as the way he scores goals. There was, in his decent and uncomplicated fashion, only one way he could put in words what it meant to be there. He said, 'I'm one of the best twenty-two players in the country.'

It was still a new feeling for him –and a very good feeling indeed. I asked how it had felt when he knew he'd been picked.

'It took a while to sink in. It's three or four weeks' agonising, nail-biting – then I saw it on the teletext . . . just great.'

So what had Robson said to him?

'He's not said much. He's just said, I've brought you here to do a job, and I won't be frightened to put you on. That's all. But he's a decent manager, he'll listen to you – and the other players, they've all given me confidence. Being with them a couple of days at Burnham Beeches, you don't get to talk to many people properly. But here, being here for three or four weeks now, you're getting to know them – you get to know the insides and outsides of life. You think to yourself, OK – I'm the same as everybody else.'

Did he miss home, being away this long?

'I keep ringing my girlfriend up – it's nice to hear a woman's voice. I keep telling her now, it's only nineteen days to go, eighteen, seventeen . . . it's a bit hard, like – you enjoy the meals from home. All I'm doing now is eating soup and pasta – when I get back it'll be a good fish'n'chips, and a pint of bitter.'

What about Genoa coming after him?

'Well, I've not had no calls or nothing – but I think I'd tell them no, really. I'm happy where I am. Obviously Barnesy, some of these others, they've got to be on outstanding money, 'cos of the clubs they're at – and I think if any club in Britain came in for me, I'd have to have a serious think about it. But as long as I'm happy, that's all that matters; there's other things than money . . . I know money's a big part of it, it can secure your future – but I'm earning a steady wage to keep me going till I finish.'

And after that?

'I'd like to stay in the game, just playing amateur football – I'm too soft to be a manager.'

Then I asked what he knew about Egypt.

'Not a lot. I know they play five at the back, it'll be hard to break down. We'll see what we can do.'

And I asked what was he like, immediately before a game.

'I try not to speak to anybody, really. I just like to keep my head down, concentrate – get my shinpads on at twenty to three, get taped up and ready. Though since I've been here I've been shaking hands, geeing everyone on as we go out – I don't know if it's changing me. At the Wolves I just sit down, shake my legs, wait to get out.'

Any superstitions?

'Not really. I kiss my shirt three times on the back, I don't know why – I think the first time I did that I got a hat-trick, I've been doing it ever since. And I like to carry the No. 9, I feel strong in it. But wearing 21 here, I dunno – it doesn't matter, just being here'll do, 21, 12, 3, you don't mind so long as you're here. And, touch wood, I've not stopped scoring goals – it's not stopped since I went to Wolves. I scored against Tunisia, last ten minutes, and I've scored four here (in the local friendlies) – so I feel really confident, the way it's going on.'

But what is confidence?

'You tell me . . . confidence is just going out there and putting it in the net. That's all it is to me.'

Robson's Tornado, in formation with one other, made two low, window-shaking passes over the hotel. Barnes grumbled, 'Imagine if that was us. It'd be, what you doing going for a fucking ride?'

Some of the players watched Royal Ascot in the games room; I sat with David Platt outside. We talked, as I'd talked with Bull, about how it was to be an England new boy at Italia '90.

Platt had just turned twenty-four, so he was nearly ten years younger than Bryan Robson – going on for him against Holland was his sixth cap, compared to Robson's eighty-three.

The manager said he'd chosen Platt over McMahon in that game because he'd wanted to keep Gullit shut down; but, at the same time, he'd wanted a goalscorer too. Whereas now, against Egypt, McMahon would start, he wanted that tenacity in the middle – so Platt was on the bench.

Platt said when he went out against Holland, 'My concentration took over any nerves I might have had, 'cos I was marking such an influential player. But to replace Pop is important in itself – everybody knows about Pop, he's been there for ten years, everybody knows how important he is. So to go on for him – it was tremendous.'

Platt went to college for a year when he left school, hoping for a couple of A-levels so he could get into physiotherapy. 'That was what was in my mind – though when I look back on it, I don't think I was clever enough to be a physiotherapist. Then anyway, the opportunity arose with Manchester United. I was seventeen, I still had a year to run at college – but it was something I'd always wanted to do. I thought if I didn't make it, I could always go back to studying – but if I did another year studying then, I'd miss the chance in football.'

It didn't work out at United. He did a year as a YTS, then got a year's contract – but six months into it, Crewe came in for him, and United advised him to go. 'Obviously, going from United to Crewe Alexandra was a lot of steps down clubwise – but it was a step up too, because it meant I got first team football.' So he was there three years – then, two seasons ago, he moved to Aston Villa.

When he went out for his first cap against Italy at Wembley 'there was a lot of talk, a lot of publicity, 'cos I was getting the goals – but I thought Italy had come a bit too early for me, I expected to be in the B squad. Then we played Everton live on the telly on the Sunday, and he was naming his squad on the Monday, and I got a couple of goals, we won 6–2 – so I think maybe that swayed it.'

He said of being in the World Cup now, 'Obviously playing at Wembley, there's a lot of attention – but when you come out here, and you play the Dutch . . . I was aware afterwards, not during, 'cos your concentration's so high, but afterwards – that game's gone out to so many people, it's got world attention. Everybody's watching. Like, you go down to the training ground, and all the press that's there – yesterday I've spoken to half a dozen Italian press, and it's unnatural to you, because back home you know your reporters – the most I've ever faced is a dozen. Then all of a sudden it's a hundred, and they're like vultures, it's like flies round shit – as soon as there's something that might be a story, 'cos you've come on against the Dutch, *whoooph* . . . I said I'd speak to one, one I knew from Birmingham, and let him pass it round to them all, 'cos they all look after each other – then it's on his head.'

So I asked how he felt about the Dutch half-hour.

'I feel good about it, obviously. I'm never one to go round saying I've done this, I've done that, not in public – but I'll go back home proud of the fact that I had to stop Gullit, that I had to go out and play in that game. I was pleased with my performance; more than that, the manager was pleased – it means a lot to me. And the press can go on, but it's not just the press, it's everybody back home, they know what I did – I haven't let anybody down. So it'll be nice to look back on it, that I went out in a World Cup game at twenty-four years of age, and replaced the skipper – because in all honesty, I didn't expect to play out here at all. I expected to be just a squad member. I was very surprised, very pleased to be on the bench against the Irish – I didn't think I would be.'

So David Platt would, in the end, be doing far more than he'd ever dreamt of when he got on that plane back on 25 May. Aston Villa had bought him from Crewe for £200,000 –

after Italia '90, they were turning down an offer from Fiorentina worth £5,000,000.

Now, in advance of this unforeseen elevation, he was modest about his place. He said, 'There's nothing I want more than to play from the start, in every game – but you're one of the twenty-two. When the press all come and say I'm going to replace Bryan Robson, I'm genuine when I say I want Bryan Robson to be fit, because I genuinely do. Sure, I think I've come here on the strength of what Bobby Robson thinks David Platt can do – and obviously I'd be delighted to play, now I'm here. But that doesn't mean you want to see players injured. If Pop's fit, then Pop should play.'

But Pop wasn't fit – and it was Steve McMahon who had the midfield place against Egypt, not Platt.

'I can understand the manager's thinking. He's playing with a lot of players who are good going forward, John Barnes, Chrissie Waddle, Paul Gascoigne. Of course I feel confident that I could do a job, and hold the midfield – and that's what you've got to do if you're playing with Paul, because he's very talented, but he's going forward all the time so someone's got to sit in for him. And maybe that's more natural for Steve than for me.'

I asked what it was like, playing alongside Gazza.

'As long as you do hold, it's all right. My tendency is to go forward, so it can be difficult – even in that half-hour I was tempted, I was going up a little bit – and that's my game, I like going forward, I like getting in the box. But in international football if we both go forward, we'll get exposed – so Steve's game's more suited to holding in that way. And I'm disappointed, yeah, but then, you always know he might play Steve. So you put that behind you, and you go out there – because in the first minute Paul, or Steve, or Steve Bull, any one of them could get injured, and then I'm on. I mightn't play ninety minutes, but I might play eighty-nine – so you've got to be concentrating, you can't waste time being disappointed. I know there's players at home at Villa, or Crewe, I've spoken to them – every one of them would sooner be where I am now.'

Just waiting and hoping for his chance . . . which, when it came, he would take with a vengeance.

*

No question about one young footballer who was enjoying himself in Italy . . . Gazza spilt gleefully out of the games room and announced, 'On Your Toes, eight to one.'

Platt asked, 'How much?'

'Hundred pounds.'

Lineker the bookie went past, looking gutted.

Platt said he knew about the gee-gees – his girlfriend's brother works in a stable, and he owns a horse himself. But he said even if someone called him and said he could put his mortgage on a horse, he'd still not bet more than a hundred – whereas Gazza, in Platt's affectionately succinct phrase, was 'a daft cunt'. He didn't, Platt said, know the first thing about the horses.

And the firm of Shilton and Lineker didn't need to feel too bad – after all, what Gazza'd won today, he'd lost the day before. He'd gone into the games room, asked Peter Beardsley what horse looked likely in the next race, and then – to a mixture of amusement and horror – put £400 on it. He lost. So then he went £250 each way on the next race . . . and lost that too.

But the boredom, after twenty-six days in one place, compounded with the cyclical tension of the games coming and going, and a morose aggravation at the attentions and inventions of the press – was beginning to find outlets in stranger forms of behaviour than Gazza's impulse betting.

Two nights before the Egypt game, Woods and Butcher went to dinner with all their Umbro gear on inside out. They had their coffee first, then dessert – and so on backwards, right through the menu.

Tonight, they planned on having their buddies the waiters fill wine bottles with mineral water for them, and set them out in ice buckets on their table to wind the manager up. And they'd go into dinner in suits and ties, and all the gear – then surreptitiously hand over their trousers to an accomplice on the staff. Half-way through the meal they'd then go, phew, hot in here – they'd get up, walk over to hang their jackets on the pegs, and have nothing on below the waist but their jockstraps . . .

Like Butcher said, 'Anything to ease the boredom.'

Gazza bounced around, frantic for someone to play table tennis with him.

In the games room, Lineker idly played trick shots on the pool table.

People played cards for hours, and hours.

Robson came back from his Tornado ride – he'd been fifty miles out to sea, flown at 800 mph at low level, and looked like the happiest kid in town.

Unlike Steve McMahon. He sat alone with a coffee in the bar – and he looked so tense, so coiled up about going out to play again tomorrow, he was virtually gnawing on the table.

John Barnes wasn't a happy man either.

The *Mirror*'d run a groundless and hurtful piece of cod psychological claptrap about him, that suggested he didn't turn it on for England because his mum used to whack him when he was a kid.

So, I asked, was John Barnes disturbed?

'Disturbed by the fucking press, I tell you.'

He'd done an interview for some offbeat Channel 4 programme a while back, and they'd tried to speculate in it that because of the way he was brought up, he was spoilt. He'd said no – if he was naughty, his mum used to slap him like any other kid. So the *Mirror*'d got hold of this, and turned it into, 'MUM'S BEATINGS STILL HAUNT JOHN'.

'They call it a secret video, I mean, really – if you'd have watched Channel 4 you'd have seen it. But that's how ridiculous the whole thing's got. You know that stupid story about the girl – I don't even know what she looks like. Most of the players don't. And they talk about, "at an official disco players mingled with the hostesses" – there's been no official disco bloody anywhere, we've just stayed right here. But it's been dominating our World Cup, this stuff, unfortunately – and it's a stupid situation. Just stupid.'

So I said, let's talk football. Did he enjoy the Dutch game?

'I enjoyed the first sixty minutes. After that they took Chris off. For the first half-hour Chris had a free role, inside right, right wing, wherever he wanted, and I was playing down the middle – and we were causing them a lot of problems. But since we didn't have a left winger, their right back was going forward a lot, unmarked. Now he wasn't causing us that much trouble – but they thought he was, so they moved Chris out left to stop his runs, which was ridiculous. To put Chris out there just to run up and down with this right back and stop him playing, rather than thinking, we're causing them more problems than they are us – Chris's threat was nullified. Then when they took Chris off they put me out there, and my threat was nullified, then it's me just running up and down – and that's not my game. But it's the same old thing. For the first half-hour it was brilliant, I was in a position where I could get involved, and run around, and Chris was free – but rather than being positive and saying, OK, if we're going to have a man free, then they're going to have someone free too, so be it – I mean, you can't have it all ways, you can't have men free, and have all their men marked too . . .'

The manager's too cautious?

'He was in that instance. I think so, anyway, definitely. We could have done more going forward. We still had a spare man at the back, so even if the right back did go forward, there was someone there to deal with it. He was running into a position where all he was going to do was cross, he wasn't going to score. And you've got to realise that teams are going to get crosses in against you, they're going to get free men – but we should have free men too, rather than saying, because he's free you've got to mark him.'

The manager holds you back?

Barnes stumbled for a moment. 'No, not necess . . . it's just, not . . . not physically. Not . . . I don't think he means to. But I just feel . . . I feel the way we're asked to play definitely does. Like Ireland, for example, me and Chris were coming back on Ray Houghton and Kevin Sheedy – and a few instances I was looking at us when we're under pressure and I'm thinking, we've got the goalkeeper and nine players defending here – and Gary Lineker isolated up front. And you don't help yourself like that, do you?'

Barnes said he didn't know how it would go against Egypt – but he did know Butcher wasn't playing, and that we were back to 4–4–2. He said, 'We don't know what to expect from them – three right backs, no right back, one right back, no left wing – and that's the problem. 4–4–2, same old thing, static positions – you play these other teams, and you don't know where people are going to run. That's why a lot of them get free – sometimes they only play one up front, so in effect they've got six in midfield. And then because we play 4–4–2 – 4–2–4, supposedly, but it's really 4–4–2 – you've got four at the back marking one, and they're used to staying there, and we're getting run ragged everywhere else.'

Gazza wandered by looking restless – he'd won on another horse, but he wasn't interested in that any more. He started knocking the ball across the table tennis table on his own, a uniquely futile activity. I asked him if he'd been happy after the Holland game.

Barnes said, 'He's never happy.'

'Never happy, me.' He sang, 'Barmy Barmy Barnesy Barnesy,' and tried to hit the ping pong ball into a glass of water from five or six yards. He missed. 'Oh shit. I've got to go and get it now.'

I went back to the Dutch game.

'Paul Gascoigne was man of the match. That's why he's been chirpy all week. Talking to the press and everything – he slaughters them, but as soon as he has a good game, he's their best friend.'

'Bollocks. Paul Gascoigne *never* speaks to the fuckin' press. *Never*.'

'He never talks to anyone if they give him a bollocking. But he plays well, he's man of the match, better than Ruud Gullit – then he's running around being chirpy all right.'

'Thank you, John. Always chirpy.'

Maybe winning on the gee-gees helped a bit.

'He wins money on everything, horses, football.'

Not yesterday.

'Yeah, but I'm up £600 today. That's good.'

He was a grand up on the football, too – he'd backed Cameroon to get 1–0 over Argentina, among others. 'And the linesman denied me £600 last night, that Czech goal.'

'He was offside,' Barnes grinned.

'Was he fuck.'

He started playing solo table tennis with the bat instead of the ball, just chucking it across the table. Barnes and I sat talking about the injustices of life to a soundtrack of clattering wood . . . Maradona's handball against the Russians, Maradona getting Hagi booked, that suspiciously disallowed Czech goal. Barnes said, 'Did you see Valderrama get stretchered off yesterday? And five minutes later he just walks back on – fuck-all wrong with him. I don't like it.'

Then he called out, 'No, Gazza, I'm not playing table tennis with you. You can't play table tennis in your flip flops. The manager said.'

I asked one more time about the trouble with Barnesy – did he play less well for his country than his club?

'What I said still stands – even more so now. Look at the Holland game. We're causing problems, and all of a sudden . . . see, had it been the other way round, after thirty minutes I'd have gone to mark the right back. And the rest of the match I'd have been running up and down. But Chris had to do it – so at least I enjoyed sixty, seventy minutes of it. But after that I was just marking, basically.'

He said, 'Take Gary Lineker. His game's about scoring goals. So if he doesn't get a chance to score, you can't criticise him – because whatever else he might be doing, he's not in the team to do that, he's not in the team to be beating three players, or to be tackling back and chasing. He's in the team to score goals. Give him a chance, and he'll score. But me, I'm in the team to create chances, and to do things going forward. And if I'm not given the opportunity to do that, I'm not going to be effective. I'm not in the team to . . . well, as it turns out, that's what I have been doing, tracking back with the right back. But if that's the way the games are going to go . . .'

And the trouble with Barnesy came down to the crunch.

He said, if that was the way it was going to go, 'I think we'd be better off to play someone else in that position, if he's going to run up and down with the full back. It's like asking Gary Lineker to do it. You might as well not have him in the side. And you might as well not have me in the side, if that's all that's going to happen. Like I've said, if a cross comes in, or a ball comes through, there's only one person can clear it out. So how many defenders do we need?'

And how clear can it get? He was, I said, unhappy.

'Yes.' Long pause. 'I'm unhappy with the job I'm asked to do.'

*

It had been harsh and muggy weather all afternoon. I got a ride back into Cagliari with two BBC boys, feeling harsh and muggy myself.

Grim premonitions sat heavy on my heart. We'd woken up against Holland, but it was a false dawn – we were, now, to be sent back to sleep again. Wright and Parker in for Butcher and Stevens, fine – they might be faster, more inventive – but still it was, in Barnes's words, 'the same old thing'.

Bobby Robson is a kind, courteous, and decent man. But he's also a man for whom World War II ran through six central years of his childhood; and a man who, when he started to play professional football as a teenager in the early fifties, would have been coached and surrounded in the game by men who fought in that war. It's the working class who are, after all, the poor bloody infantry – the same people who have football in their blood, and in their souls. And in the steel for the game in his heart, he'd learnt to think of it as war.

And Robson loved skill, he loved class, he stood by Barnes and Waddle, and he kept on picking them – they had over fifty caps each. And he looked with a weary distaste, verging on contempt, at the hoofing mess of the Irish, or of so much of the First Division which the Irish game so much more nearly epitomised than the ball-to-feet quality he wanted to coax from his own men.

But at the core of his wish to play football – to play as others could in Europe – there still lay two insoluble contradictions.

Firstly, he loved to win, he was desperate to win – but he was at least as much terrified of losing. At the press conferences that morning he'd said, Egypt was a game we must not lose. It was a game we had to win – but what he stressed first and most was, it was a game *we must not lose*.

But with Group F the way it was we were, in effect, going into the first knock-out game of Italia '90 – because what use was a draw? Who wanted to risk a Dutch–Irish draw in Palermo too, and see all four sides jammed on the same points, the same goals, and then FIFA drawing lots to see who carried on? (What the good doctor Ahmed El-Mokadem called derisively, 'World Cup bingo'.)

So who wanted to risk that? – especially with the certainty fixed in the hearts of many English, that we and our fans were unwelcome guests, so that if it came to drawing balls from a

FIFA glass bowl, one of those balls would be square, and the English would conveniently be drawn to go home . . . how, in these circumstances, could we go up against the Egyptians *fearful of losing*?.

And the second contradiction: that, in the straitjacket conservatism of his Englishness, and of the English game, Robson saw the sweeper thing as defensive, and saw 4–4–2 with two wingers as bold and attacking. Yet then, all caution, he told the players who we needed to be bold and attacking, that they weren't free to do so . . . so that Barnes and Waddle were unhappy; and what in theory was offensive, became scrambling-back defensive.

And I could see us losing. I hated the thought, but I could see us actually losing it. Robson was a good man, and his players were good men too – they were generous, they were good company, they fought hard, they gave 110 per cent . . . they were, in short, English, and the approach was all played out, and I could see us losing.

Italy, Germany, Brazil – even Belgium, even Cameroon – *that* was football.

Whereas us – we were history.

We were resolute still, perhaps, but we were fearful too. We were padlocked in ways of thinking we knew didn't work any more – yet we were too fractiously, obstinately, nervily bulldog-headed to change, and then stay changed.

The empire was gone, and the world was passed on. The colonies became independent, Europe became a Community – and in 1953, the Hungarians came to Wembley to wallop the founders of football 6–3. And did we learn?

No. We stayed on our island, growling behind our nukes with our thuggish dirty streets, our polluted beaches, our hospitals where the rain comes through the roof, and our schools that can't afford to buy books – we stayed on our island with our fading industries, and our 4–4–2.

In the BBC car we drove over the brow of the hill above Sarroch, down past the steel jungles of the refinery and the chemical plant, towards the causeway across the bay and into Cagliari. The evening had grown muggier than ever; a fuggy haze of grimy grey-blue sat heavily down over the sea, and the town beyond it. There was no line where water stopped, or sky started; Cagliari had vanished.

All you could make out through the bleary murk was the four blazing flares of the floodlights of the Sant'Elia – four eerie spectres hovering on the dim horizon where the Egyptians were training.

Still, what have I got to worry about? I could be a Scotland fan . . . great parties, no question – but then you have to go and watch that unbelievable, that heart-breaking team.

Five times in succession, this nation of five million had qualified for the World Cup – a record that included, this time, getting to Italy ahead of France. Yet after that, they'd never got past the first round – a saga of failure by turns glorious and ignominious.

In Germany '74, they got draws with Brazil and Yugoslavia, and went home unbeaten on goal difference alone.

But in Argentina '78, Peru beat them 3–1. Then they drew with Iran, and only managed that thanks to an Iranian own goal – a national nightmare rendered doubly frustrating by a heroic 3–2 defeat of the Dutch, who went on to the finals.

In Spain '82, they avoided similar embarrassment by tonking New Zealand 5–2, and then had the audacity to score first against Brazil – who, stung, promptly scored four.

And in Mexico '86, after narrow defeats at the hands of the Germans and the Danes, they still had a chance of a third-place passage, when a Uruguayan was sent off after just fifty-five seconds – but against ten men, they failed to take it.

Now in Italy they were at it again, a befuddling mix of bravery and incompetence. Beaten by Costa Rica, victors over Sweden, they needed a point off Brazil – and they held out for eighty-two minutes, with Jim Leighton making a fine save off Romario, before falling victim to the most abject bad luck.

First, Leighton stopped a fierce twenty-five-yard shot from Alemao, but failed to hold it – and Muller tapped in the rebound. Leighton beat the ground with his fists, he kicked the goalpost in rage and misery . . . then, in the dying seconds, Mo Johnston fired a shot from close range that you'd have backed to go in from the second it left his boot. Yet somehow, Taffarel threw his body across it and flung out a hand, got a miraculous touch, and the ball flew wide – it was an awesome save. Johnston lay face down on the turf in an agonised eternity of disbelief . . . I felt like I could hear the grief of Glasgow from 2,000 miles away. Brazil 1, Scotland 0.

And you might think it the fiercest injustice, that this small country should so consistently be singled out for such raised hopes, such shattered expectations – but since when was football about justice?

Football's about not getting beat by the likes of Costa Rica . . . whose manager Bora Milutinovic knew his job. After a playing career in Yugoslavia, France, Switzerland and Mexico, he'd managed Mexico to the quarter-finals in '86 – but his achievement now was even greater.

In Genoa, it was Sweden 1, Costa Rica 2 – and they joined Brazil in the second round.

All evening it threatened rain; an hour after midnight, the threat was made good.

I was getting into bed – but then I heard the chanting begin again, the raucous belchy yelling, and I got up to go see what I could see.

There was a mobile snack van on the corner of the little park outside the bus station, selling chips and wurst and *panini*. Maybe twenty English were gathered there, stuffing chips in their faces; and they'd been drinking too, though you'd not say they were legless.

Most had their shirts off; they were a sorry-looking lot, with their mottled paunches rolling over the tops of their mutant's puke shorts, and their ill-fitting jeans. Two of them were particularly weedy – really scrawny specimens, noisily leaching manhood off their bulkier breathren. Some had skinhead baldness; others longer and lank, rain-flattened hair. The Chelsea antiques fence was among them; and he was holding shirts and umpiring, or seconding, in a singular and neanderthal exhibition of truly oafish machismo.

Pairs of men ran together and chest-butted each other, arms loose and jerking at their sides, in repeated little sumo-style charges. Rain-drenched guts and shoulders whacked and slapped together, as the others gathered round each slovenly contest to chant,

Chaaahhm - pi - oh - naze

Chaaahhm - pi - oh - naze

They toppled about jeering and bawling, bodies thunking together, flesh plashing against unhealthy flesh. The rank artificial light of the snack bar shone out over them, and on the cracked and litter-strewn paving; Sards and a few police watched, as you'd watch disturbed and lumbering apes caged in a zoo. And all the while the rain hammered down, and vast lightning flashed obscurely in dense clouds. Thunder approached, crackling and booming.

It was primeval, debased, drunk – a scene from the urban apocalypse. It was,

Inngg - ger - luh-uhnd
Inngg - ger - luh-uhnd

All played out.

The next morning there were QPR fans outside La Perla. Why, they asked, had Robson taken so long to play Paul Parker?

'Look, we know we can all pick the team. But it's not who plays, it's how. And I *liked* that system against Holland. But every time the Dutch had the ball, you watch 'em, just watch 'em – the whole lot of 'em drop back. Robson's trouble's he's too bloody nervous – we've got the players, so *why don't we play?* I mean, I can understand, the shit he gets – but *why don't we go forward?*'

'Bold stuff,' said another, 'that sweeper. Bold – or stupid. Thin line . . .'

'The players liked our support last Saturday, did they? Well it was great, the atmosphere – but Gazza's the only one who shows it. He's the only one who thanks us. We pay all this money to come here – they could come over at the end and say thanks, couldn't they?'

'Robson did right though, the way he's brought Gazza in. Six months back he was an immature jerk. He's handled him right.'

Word among them was that Gazza'd gone up to Van Basten during the game and said, 'How much are you on a week then?'

*

La Prensa in Bogota announced, 'Rincon's cry was the cry of all Colombians. We were so excited we prayed, laughed, cried and celebrated.'

Pagina 12 in Buenos Aires was less sure of itself, on matters of national pride: 'The Argentinian team is a fat lady whose lovers will now abandon her.' Of Maradona they said, 'Now it's God's knee.'

In Udine at five, a strangely spineless Uruguay scraped past South Korea 1–0. True, they hit the woodwork in the first minute of each half; but that was about all they hit, even when the time-wasting and tackle-happy Koreans were down to ten men in the last twenty minutes. They finally managed to score in the second minute of injury time, but they barely deserved it – and though they'd twice been Champions in 1930 and 1950, this was now the first World Cup game that they'd won since 1970. Their dubious reward in the second round was a trip to Rome, to meet Italy.

In Verona, meanwhile, King Juan Carlos and Queen Sophia turned up to watch their steadily improving Spanish side win Group E. They beat the Belgians 2–1; Michel's penalty, after his hat-trick against the Koreans, took him to the top of the goalscorers' table, ahead of West Germany's Rudi Völler.

The Belgians had a penalty too, but Enzo Scifo hit the crossbar – and Spain deserved the win. Still, both sides looked good, disciplined and skilful – and as the Belgians were through anyhow, it would have been foolhardy to read too much into their defeat. Guy Thys, the Belgian manager, said, 'I'm very satisfied. We were in command in the second half, with five new players. I don't think we have to be afraid of anybody.'

And whoever topped Group F would find them waiting in Bologna.

The evening of the 21st was warm and dry, the horizons burning orange as the sun went down. The helicopters went round and round overhead. The stadium was half empty; there were only maybe 3,500 English left on the island anyway. But the flags were still there – Blackburn, Burnley, Bootle, Newcastle, Isle of Wight.

One said bluntly, 'Moynihan Is A Traitor'.

And another announced contentedly, 'Greavsie: Sphinx–Nil. You can't say pharoah than that'.

The Egyptian fans were one small block dressed all in white – a shipload of Egyptian navy cadets who'd been given leave, and the use of their boat, to follow their side between the islands until the first round was done.

As usual, they all had a flag to wave. Everyone else, you thought, was so festive, so colourful, and here they were, with their fluttering black, red, and white – while ours sat flagless, because at the searches on your way into the stadium, the *carabinieri* stripped the poles out of the spines of your Union Jack. If you were English you could drape it – but you couldn't wave it . . .

And off we go again.

And Egypt have more of the ball . . .

And who'd be a football fan? The doubts, the anxieties, the fears . . . I wondered again if I could bring myself to write it down any more, as I sat there yearning for us to play, and to win.

Pearce made a good run up the left; Lineker was obstructed, but the referee ignored it. He got through again; we won a free-kick, and it led to a corner. The argy-bargy in the box was sullen and tempestuous.

I was on the edge of the press box; the England fans to my right were in a rage of hope and criticism.

'Get in front of him, get wider, c'mon, *c'mon* . . . who wants it, *who wants it*? Barnes, get *in* man, you poof – where's the support? C'mon Stevie, get in there – you gotta look, you're not fucking looking . . .'

As another pass faded a vivid Geordie voice sweetly sighed, a groan of soft disgust, '*Oh dear* . . .'

It was flat back four again, and another squashed midfield. Lineker and Bull spent long periods spectating – the Egyptians were playing for the draw, just rolling it around, and there were too many back passes by far. As David Lacey put it, their football 'drifted back and forth across their own half like the shifting, whispering sands'. I even began to sympathise with Jack Charlton . . .

It was scrappy and unconvincing, twenty minutes of nothing – the subs were warming up already. McMahon at least was hurrying and harrying; and when Barnes got the ball it was, 'Skin him, *gwooaahhn*' . . . but he never seemed to.

And a man could die of boredom watching this – if it didn't matter so much . . . then, slowly, the Egyptians seemed to realise, if they went forward they might win – they had more of the ball, and they were getting in the crosses. At one scary moment the Geordie next door to me whimpered a little 'Ah', as with the pain and fear of a man under torture . . . and their next attack was scarier yet; Parker slipped up, he let a man free into the box – and the Geordie positively whined with alarm.

But then Gazza brought it away on the sprint – and the whine converted into a groaning roar of desire, '*Do it for me Gazza . . .*'

Bull was trying hard to do it too. Three times he fished half-shots out of nothing, off balance with no real chance – but still he pushed and lunged, just desperate to pelt it in, the bobbling ball flim-flamming in front of him among the knots of defenders, and still he kept on trying . . . and so did Gazza. Twice he beat one man, two, three down the wing – twice he danced through throngs of Egyptians massed on the edge of the area, just standing there bewitched by his swaying, tripping, shimmying little runs – but it came to nothing. There were too many of them, and none of us.

An Egyptian long shot damn near skimmed in, Shilton touching it uncomfortably away. At the other end, Lineker's neat one-two sent Parker through – but his shot was pushed aside. Someone gave Barnes a good hacking, and Gazza near went mental, asking the ref in no uncertain terms, did he need a visit to the optician . . . and we reached half-time, bored and goalless.

In Palermo the Dutch were 1–0 up on the Irish – Gullit, who'd scored, was looking a yard quicker. Out came the calculators and the second round schedules for more frantic perming of the last-ditch possibilities. If it stayed this way Holland were top, Ireland were out, and England and Egypt were in FIFA's glass bowl for the lottery draw between second place in Genoa, and third place in the dens of Germany's Milan, or Brazilian Turin . . .

The second half began with England attacking again. Bull came close from Waddle's cross; Parker skinned two men, and another cross was just barely hoiked away. 'Get it *sorted*,' wailed the Geordie.

And Paul Gascoigne and Mark Wright sorted it. Walker went forward, and was brought down; Gazza's curling chip of a free-kick, perfectly weighted, floated over for Wright to rise and head (as they say) unerringly home . . .

We're on the march with Bobby's army
We're all going to Italy
And we'll really shake 'em up
When we win the World Cup
'Cos England are the greatest football team

But not on this showing they weren't.

Egypt were coming forward now at least as much as we were. The back line was solid, and Parker looked good pushing up; McMahon was everywhere, and Gazza was brilliant – but Waddle and Barnes were invisible again, Bull was struggling for space and touch, and Lineker looked like he was hurting.

The fans screamed at Barnes, 'Express yourself!' But he never really did. And when Waddle lifted a hand at the ref one time instead of playing on, it was, 'Get off the park, you shit.'

In Palermo, Niall Quinn got one back for the Irish – so we had to keep hold of the win now.

Three minutes after Quinn's goal 200 miles away, Peter Shilton made sure that we did. The ball fell to Hani Ramzi close to goal, and Shilton fell like a rock on his quickly snapped shot . . . and the last minutes dragged out in agony, as the fans howled cheerfully,

England, England
Top of the group
Top of the group

Much good it would do us later, if we played like this again. It wasn't as bad as the Irish game, and two Egyptians were booked for time-wasting – they'd come for the draw, and their lack of ambition had undone them. But still, you could hardly say we took it to them.

England 1, Egypt 0. Holland 1, Ireland 1.

Top of the group – and Belgium waited in Bologna.

*

For the first time football, rather than fantasy scandals, took England to the front page – the front page of, who else, the *Sun*:

> ENGLAND GIVE 'EM A PHAROAH STUFFING
> Our soccer heroes shook off the Sphinx jinx and anNILEated the Egyptians . . . as England stormed to victory in Cagliari, Sardinia.

And of course we didn't storm, we just grittily stumbled – but the tabloids went briefly loopy on the glory-glory angle anyway, their jubilation as wildly unrealistic as their past relentless criticism.

> WE'VE MADE IT!
>
> THAT'S ALL WRIGHT!
>
> HERO MARK
>
> WORLD CUP GLORY FOR ROBBO MEN

But once you got past the headlines, more balanced and worried voices could be heard in many quarters.

Harry Harris in the *Mirror*: 'The bitter truth is that until Wright struck, England did precious little.'

Jeff Powell in the *Mail*: 'Had Bobby Robson persevered with his adoption of a modern sweeper system, England might have out-manouevred the North Africans . . . but England regressed into their old-fashioned ways.'

And Stuart Jones in *The Times*: 'Rather than the flexible and fluent unit of last Saturday, England appeared to be disjointed and uninspired . . . Barnes, once more showing a singular lack of urgency on the left, looked as though he required permission to take on an opponent.'

And I don't see a lot to disagree with there. Sure, the Egyptians didn't make it easy – but it's not meant to be easy, is it? Compared to the Germans and others, it was, in short, a dog of a way to come top, in a dog of a group.

Group F had seen a meagre total of only seven goals scored, and five draws in six games – whereas in the German group there'd been twenty-one goals, and fourteen in three of the others. The best you can say is, England toughed it out – they were England.

But when you looked at what had gone on elsewhere, both on and off the pitch, Cagliari – bar ninety minutes against Holland – had been no kind of party at all.

To make matters worse, one of the coaches in a convoy bringing fans to the stadium crashed; one English boy died.

The FA's good side came out, Kelly and others looking after the boy's parents when they came over; and the FA paid for their accommodation. The players were good too, visiting the fifteen or so injured in hospital.

But right there and then, at the Sant'Elia after the game, the atmosphere was so grim you'd have thought we'd been disqualified, rather than struggling out on top.

I walked down a white-washed concrete corridor curving through the bowels of the stadium, and came to a gaggle of TV crews outside the dressing rooms. In an alcove by a backdrop board bearing the names of FIFA's sponsors, next to a phone and a trolley of medical kit, was a camera position marked Flash Interview. Round the corner, the players ducked out towards the dark, fenced-off bus park; I followed through, and saw a stony-faced McMahon being hassled by five guys with dictaphones as he tried to get on the bus. 'I'm sorry,' he said, 'I've nothing to say.'

'But it's the World Cup,' they pleaded.

'Too right it is. And you treat us properly, you might get stories.'

He vanished into the bus.

It was strangely quiet; it was entirely joyless. We were top of the group . . . and stumbling harassed and uneasy out of Cagliari.

When I asked one of the men from the qualities how he felt about it, he said, 'Relieved. It would have been very unpleasant if he'd lost. Especially with that team.'

And the players hunched through like haunted men, journos scuffling in their path for quotes; a BBC crew panted after them too, swinging the light and the camera on each one in turn – 'This one, this one' – and shoving and pushing at the bus door as Rob Bonnet hectically lobbed in his questions, in snatched and accelerated bursts of words.

'Howdidthegamego?'

'Whatd'youthinkofBelgiumnextroundPaul?'

The answers were few and spartan; the bus park had a thrumming undertone of soured relationships – and of men who should have been happy with their progress, knowing instead how that progress had been difficult and ungainly. And anyway, so what, when a twenty-year-old boy had died?

Mark Wright was backed up against a wall by the biggest pack; but then, he'd talk all right, and fair enough – he'd just scored his first goal for England, in his twenty-sixth game.

Robson came out with his arm round the shoulders of El-Gohary, the Egyptian coach – a typically decent and considerate gesture.

I asked Rob Bonnet later what he'd got and he said, 'Very little.' He said he'd tried to get Robson, to ask about the bus crash – he'd wanted, he said, to get a quick, 'Good-result-on-the-night-but-sad-about-the-news-of-the-accident-Bobby'. . . which seems to me a pretty base and invasive sort of question. What on earth could Robson have said, except yes on both counts?

But there you go, that's football management 1990 – you carry the hopes of the nation, and become a universal spokesman in times happy, and times sad.

Back in the press centre, the monitors showed FIFA's general secretary Sepp Blatter do his 'clean hands' act again. As he'd done for the draw in Rome in December, he supervised the placing of plastic balls in glass bowls – then called to the bowls a nervous stewardess, who allotted second place to Ireland, and third place to the Dutch.

And no matter if their football was about as attractive as a pack of warthogs running riot in a mud bath – for Ireland to have got there at all, for the first time in their history, was achievement enough. But to have qualified now too, that was remarkable – and when did Jack Charlton ever care about points for artistic impression? He said, 'Palermo tonight will have the biggest party it's ever seen.'

But not Cagliari – not policed-to-silence Cagliari.

I went outside to catch the media bus back into town. The white tent of the press centre sat, faintly aglow, on the other side of the emptying car park; two months ago, all this had been bare dirt.

But now for Cagliari it was over, on a hot night, in a light sea breeze. The BBC truck pulled out with the last taxis and hired cars – and the phone booths stood bright-lit and empty. No one was calling from Cagliari any more.

Nice town, shame about the football . . . I turned to get on the bus, feeling sad; then I thought, fuck it.

We came top of the group, didn't we?

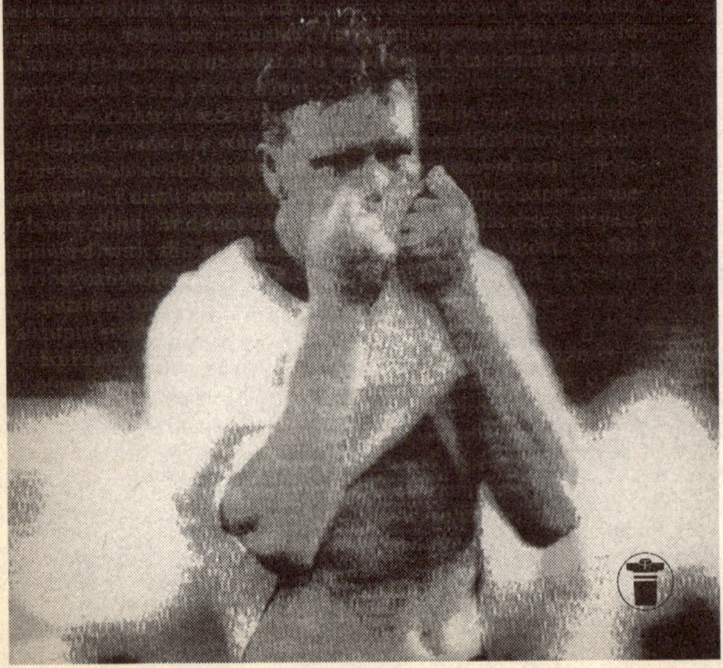